Also
by
Toni
Cade
Bambara

The Black Woman
Tales and Short Stories for Black Folk
Gorilla, My Love

The
Sea Birds Are
Still Alive

The Sea Birds Are Still Alive

Collected Stories

by
Toni Cade Bambara

Random House
New York

Copyright © 1974, 1977 by Toni Cade Bambara
All rights reserved under International and Pan-American Copyright Conventions.
Published in the United States by Random House, Inc., New York, and
simultaneously in Canada by Random House of Canada Limited, Toronto.
Manufactured in the United States of America

"The Long Night" originally appeared in *Black World,* and "Witchbird" was first
published in *Essence.*

Library of Congress Cataloging in Publication Data

Bambara, Toni Cade.
The sea birds are still alive.

CONTENTS: The organizer's wife.—The apprentice.
Broken field running.—The sea birds are still alive.—
The long night. [etc.]
I. Title.
PZ4.B2116or [PS3552.A473]   813'.5'4   76-53533
ISBN 0-394-48143-7

9 8 7 6 5 4 3 2
First Edition

CONTENTS

The
Sea Birds Are
Still Alive

THe
ORGANiZER'S
WiFe

The men from the co-op school were squatting in her garden.
Jake, who taught the day students and hassled the town school
board, was swiping at the bushy greens with his cap, dislodging
slugs, raising dust. The tall gent who ran the graphics workshop
was pulling a penknife open with his teeth, scraping rust from
the rake she hadn't touched in weeks. Old Man Boone was up
and down. Couldn't squat too long on account of the ankle
broken in last spring's demonstration when the tobacco
weights showed funny. Jack-in-the-box up, Boone snatched at
a branch or two and stuffed his pipe—crumblings of dry leaf,
bits of twig. Down, he eased string from the seams of his
overalls, up again, thrumbling up tobacco from the depths of
his pockets.

She couldn't hear them. They were silent. The whole morning stock-still, nothing stirring. The baby quiet too, drowsing
his head back in the crook of her arm as she stepped out into
the sun already up and blistering. The men began to unbend,

3

shifting weight to one leg then the other, watching her move about the jumbled yard. But no one spoke.

She bathed the baby with the little dew that had gathered on what few leaves were left on the branches crackling, shredding into the empty rain barrels. The baby gurgled, pinching her arms. Virginia had no energy for a smile or a wince. All energy summoned up at rising was focused tightly on her two errands of the day. She took her time going back in, seeing the men shift around in the heaps of tomatoes, in the snarl of the strawberry runners. Stamped her shoe against each step, carrying the baby back in. Still no one spoke, though clearly, farmers all their lives, they surely had some one thing to say about the disarray of her garden.

The young one, whose voice she well knew from the sound truck, had his mouth open and his arm outstretched as though to speak on the good sense of turning every inch of ground to food, or maybe to rant against the crime of letting it just go. He bent and fingered the brown of the poke salad that bordered the dry cabbages, his mouth closing again. Jake rose suddenly and cleared his throat, but turned away to light Old Man Boone's pipe, lending a shoulder for the old one to hunch against, cupping the bowl and holding the match, taking a long lingering time, his back to her. She sucked her teeth and went in.

When she came out again, banding the baby's carry straps around her waist, she moved quickly, stepping into the radishes, crushing unidentifiable shoots underfoot. Jake stepped back out of the way and caught his cuffs in the rake. Jake was the first in a long line to lose his land to unpaid taxes. The bogus receipts were pinned prominently as always to his jacket pocket. Signed by someone the county said did not exist, but who'd managed nonetheless to buy up Jake's farm at auction and turn it over swiftly to the granite company. She looked from the huge safety pin to the hot, brown eyes that quickly dropped. The other men rose up around her, none taller than she, though all taller than the corn bent now, grit-laden with neglect. Out of the corner of her eye, she saw a white worm work its way into the once-silky tufts turned straw, then disappear.

"Mornin," she said, stretching out her hand.

The men mumbled quickly, clearing their throats again. Boone offering a hand in greeting, then realizing she was extending not her hand but the small, round tobacco tin in it. Graham's red tobacco tin with the boy in shiny green astride an iron horse. It was Graham's habit, when offering a smoke, to spin some tale or other about the boy on the indestructible horse, a tale the smoker would finish. The point always the same—the courage of the youth, the hope of the future. Boone drew his hand back quickly as though the red tin was aflame. She curled her hand closed and went out the gate, slowly, deliberately, fixing her tall, heavy image indelibly on their eyes.

"Good-for-nuthin."

They thought that's what they heard drift back over her shoulder. Them? The tin? The young one thought he saw her pitch it into the clump of tomatoes hanging on by the gate. But no one posed the question.

"Why didn't you say somethin?" Jake demanded of his star pupil, the orator, whose poems and tales and speeches delivered from the sound truck had done more to pull the districts together, the women all said, than all the leaflets the kids cluttered the fields with, than all the posters from the co-op's graphic workshop masking the road signs, than all the meetings which not all the folk could get to.

"Why didn't you speak?" Jake shoved the young one, and for a minute they were all stumbling, dancing nimbly to avoid destroying food that could still be salvaged.

"Watch it, watch it now," Old Boone saying, checking his foot brace and grabbing the young one up, a fistful of sleeve.

"You shoulda said somethin," the tall gent spat.

"Why me?" The young one whined—not in the voice he'd cultivated for the sound truck. "I don't know her no better than yawl do."

"One of the women shoulda come," said the tall gent.

The men looked at each other, then stared down the road. It was clear that no one knew any more how to talk to the bristling girl-woman, if ever any had.

It wasn't a shift in breeze that made the women look up, faces stuck out as if to catch the rain. 'Cause there was no breeze and there'd been no rain. And look like, one of them said, there'd be no bus either. The strained necks had more to do with sound than weather. Someone coming. A quick check said all who worked in town were already gathered at the bus stop. Someone coming could only mean trouble—fire broke out somewhere, riot in town, one of the children hurt, market closed down, or maybe another farm posted. The women standing over their vegetable baskets huddled together for conference, then broke apart to jut their bodies out over the road for a look-see. The women seated atop the bags of rags or uniforms, clustered to question each other, then scattered, some standing tiptoe, others merely leaning up from the rocks to question the market women. And in that brief second, as bodies pulled upward, the rocks blotted up more sun to sear them, sting them, sicken them with. These stones, stacked generations ago to keep the rain from washing the road away, banked higher and broader by the young folk now to keep the baking earth from breaking apart.

Virginia nodded to the women, her earrings tinkling against her neck. The "Mornins" and "How do's" came scraggly

across the distance. The bus-stop plot was like an island sepa-
rated from the mainland road by shimmering sheets of heat,
by arid moats and gullies that had once been the drainage
system, dried-out craters now misshapen, as though pitted and
gouged by war.

One clear voice rising above the scattered sopranos, calling
her by name, slowed Virginia down. Frankie Lee Taylor, the
lead alto in the choir, was standing on the rocks waving, out
of her choir robes and barely recognizable but for that red-and-
yellow jumper, the obligatory ugly dress just right for the kitch-
ens in town. "Everything all right?" the woman asked for
everyone there. And not waiting for a word once Virginia's face
could be read by all, she continued: "Bus comin at all, ever?"

Virginia shrugged and picked up her pace. If the six-thirty
bus was this late coming, she thought, she could make the first
call and be back on the road in time for the next bus to town.
She wouldn't have to borrow the church station wagon after
all. She didn't want to have to ask for nothing. When she saw
Graham that afternoon she wanted the thing stitched up,
trimmed, neat, finished. Wanted to be able to say she asked
for "nuthin from nobody and didn't nobody offer up nuthin."
It'd be over with. They'd set bail and she'd pay it with the
money withheld from the seed and the fertilizer, the wages not
paid to the two students who used to help in the garden, the
money saved 'cause she was too cranky to eat, to care. Pay the
bail and unhook them both from this place. Let some other
damn fool break his health on this place, the troubles.

She'd been leaving since the first day coming, the day her
sister came home to cough herself to death and leave her there
with nobody to look out for her 'cept some hinkty cousins in
town and Miz Mama Mae, who shook her head sadly whenever
the girl spoke of this place and these troubles and these people
and one day soon leaving for some other place. She'd be going

now for sure. Virginia was smiling now and covering a whole lotta ground.

Someone was coming up behind her, churning up the loose layers of clay, the red-and-yellow jumper a mere blur in the haze of red dust. Everyone these dry, hot days looked like they'd been bashed with a giant powder puff of henna. Virginia examined her own hands, pottery-red like the hands of her cousins seen through the beauty-parlor windows in town, hands sunk deep in the pots, working up the mud packs for the white women lounging in the chairs. She looked at her arms, her clothes, and slowed down. Not even well into the morning and already her skimpy bath ruined. The lime-boiled blouse no longer white but pink.

"Here, Gin," the woman was saying. "He a good man, your man. He share our hardships, we bear his troubles, our troubles." She was stuffing money in between the carry straps, patting the chubby legs as the baby lolled in his cloth carriage. "You tell Graham we don't forget that he came back. Lots of the others didn't, forgot. You know, Gin, that you and me and the rest of the women . . ." She was going to say more but didn't. Was turning with her mouth still open, already trotting up the road, puffs of red swirling about her feet and legs, dusting a line in that red-and-yellow jumper the way Miz Mama Mae might do making hems in the shop.

Virginia hoisted the baby higher on her back and rewound the straps, clutching the money tight, flat in her fist. She thought about Miz Mama Mae, pins in her mouth, fussing at her. "What's them hanky-type hems you doin, Gin?" she'd say, leaning over her apprentice. "When ya sew for the white folks you roll them kinda stingy hems. And you use this here oldish thread to insure a quick inheritance. But when you sew for us folks, them things got to last season in and season out and many a go-round exchange. Make some hefty hems, girl, hefty."

And Virginia had come to measure her imprisonment by how many times that same red-and-yellow jumper met her on the road, faded and fading some more, but the fairly bright hem getting wider and wider, the telltale rim recording the seasons past, the owners grown. While she herself kept busting out of her clothes, straining against the good thread, outdistancing the hefty hems. Growing so fast from babe to child to girl to someone, folks were always introducing and reintroducing themselves to her. It seemed at times that the walls wouldn't contain her, the roof wouldn't stop her. Busting out of childhood, busting out her clothes, but never busting out the place.

And now the choir woman had given her the money like that and spoken, trying to attach her all over again, root her, ground her in the place. Just when there was a chance to get free. Virginia clamped her jaws tight and tried to go blank. Tried to blot out all feelings and things—the farms, the co-op sheds, the lone gas pump, a shoe left in the road, the posters promising victory over the troubles. She never wanted these pictures called up on some future hot, dry day in some other place. She squinted, closed her eyes even, 'less the pictures cling to her eyes, store in the brain, to roll out later and crush her future with the weight of this place and its troubles.

Years before when there'd been rain and ways to hold it, she'd trotted along this road not seeing too much, trotting and daydreaming, delivering parcels to and from Miz Mama Mae's shop. She could remember that one time, ducking and dodging the clods of earth chucked up by the horse's hooves. Clods spinning wet and heavy against her skirts, her legs, as she followed behind, seeing nothing outside her own pictures but that horse and rider. Trying to keep up, keep hold of the parcel slipping all out of shape in the drizzle, trying to piece together the things she would say to him when he finally turned round and saw her. She had lived the scene often enough in bed to know she'd have to speak, say something to make him hoist her up behind him in the saddle, to make him gallop her off to the new place. She so busy dreaming, she let the curve of the road swerve her off toward the edge. Mouthing the things to say and even talking out loud with her hands and almost losing the slippery bundle, not paying good enough attention. And a ball of earth shot up and hit her square in the chest and sent her stumbling over the edge into the gully. The choir organist's robe asprawl in the current that flushed the garbage down from the hill where the townies lived, to the bottom where the folks lived, to the pit where the co-op brigade made compost heaps for independence, laughing.

Graham had pulled her up and out by the wrists, pulled her against him and looked right at her. Not at the cabbage leaves or chicory on her arms, a mango sucked hairy to its pit clinging to her clothes. But looked at her. And no screen door between them now. No glass or curtain, or shrub peeked through.

"You followin me." He grinned. And she felt herself swimming through the gap in his teeth.

And now she would have to tell him. 'Cause she had lost three times to the coin flipped on yesterday morning. Had lost to the icepick pitched in the afternoon in the dare-I-don't-I boxes her toe had sketched in the yard. Had lost at supper to the shadow slanting across the tablecloth that reached her wrist before Miz Mama Mae finished off the corn relish. Had lost that dawn to the lazy lizard, suddenly quickened in his journey on the ceiling when the sun came up. Lost against doing what she'd struggled against doing in order to win one more day of girlhood before she jumped into her womanstride and stalked out on the world. I want to come to you. I want to come to you and be with you. I want to be your woman, she did not say after all.

"I want to come to the co-op school," she said. "I want to learn to read better and type and figure and keep accounts so I can get out of . . ."—this place, she didn't say—"my situation."

He kept holding her and she kept wanting and not wanting to ease out of his grip and rescue the choir robe before it washed away.

"I had five years schooling 'fore I came here," she said, talking way too loud. "Been two years off and on at the church school . . . before you came."

"You do most of Miz Mama Mae's cipherin I hear? Heard you reading the newspapers to folks in the tobacco shed. You read well."

She tried to pull away then, thinking he was calling her a liar or poking fun some way. "Cipherin" wasn't how he talked. But he didn't let go. She expected to see her skin twisted and puckered when she looked at where he was holding her. But his grip was soft. Still she could not step back.

"You been watchin me," he said with the grin again. And looking into his face, she realized he wasn't at all like she'd thought. Was older, heavier, taller, smoother somehow. But then looking close up was not like sneaking a look from the toolshed as he'd come loping across the fields with his pigeon-toed self and in them soft leather boots she kept waiting to see fall apart from rough wear till she finally decided he must own pairs and pairs of all the same kind. Yes, she'd watched him on his rounds, in and out of the houses, the drying sheds, down at the docks, after fellowship in the square. Talking, laughing, teaching, always moving. Had watched him from the trees, through windows as he banged tables, arguing about deeds, urging, coaxing, pleading, hollering, apologizing, laughing again. In the early mornings, before Miz Mama Mae called the girls to sew, she had watched him chinning on the bar he'd slammed between the portals of the co-op school door. Huffing, puffing, cheeks like chipmunks. The dark circle of his gut sucking in purple, panting out blue. Yes, she watched him. But she said none of this or of the other either. Not then.

"I want to come to night school" was how she put it. "I don't know yet what kinda work I can do for the co-op. But I can learn."

"That's the most I ever heard you talk," he was saying, laughing so hard, he loosened his grip. "In the whole three years I've been back, that's the most—" He was laughing again. And he was talking way too loud himself.

She hadn't felt the least bit foolish standing there in the drizzle, in the garbage, tall up and full out of her clothes nearly, and Graham laughing at her. Not the least bit foolish 'cause he was talking too loud and laughing too hard. And she was going to go to his school. And whether he knew it or not, he was going to take her away from this place.

Wasn't but a piece of room the school, with a shed tacked on in back for storage and sudden meetings. The furniture was bandaged but brightly painted. The chemistry equipment was old but worked well enough. The best thing was the posters. About the co-op, about Malcolm and Harriet and Fannie Lou, about Guinea-Bissau and Vietnam. And the posters done by the children, the pictures cut from magazines, the maps—all slapped up as though to hold the place together, to give an identity to the building so squat upon the land. The identity of the place for her was smells. The smell of mortar vibrating from the walls that were only wood. The smell of loam that curled up from the sink, mostly rusted metal. The green-and-brown smell rising up over heads sunk deep into palms as folks leaned over their papers, bearing down on stumps of pencil or hunks of charcoal, determined to get now and to be what they'd been taught was privilege impossible, what they now knew was their right, their destiny.

"Season after season," Graham was dictating that first night, leaning up against the maps with the ruler, "we have pulled gardens out of stones, creating something from nothing—creators."

Sweat beading on a nose to her left, a temple to her right. Now and then a face she knew from fellowship looking up as Graham intoned the statements, tapping the ruler against the table to signal punctuation traps. And she working hard, harder than some, though she never ever did learn to speak her speak as most folks finally did. But grateful just to be there, and up in front, unlike the past when, condemned by her size, she'd been always exiled in the rear with the goldfish tanks or the rabbits that always died, giving her a suspect reputation.

"The first step toward getting the irrigation plant," he continued, crashing the ruler down, "is to organize."

"Amen," said one lady by the window, never looking up from her paper, certain she would finally train herself and be selected secretary of the church board. "That way us folks can keep track of them folks" was how she'd said it when she rose to speak her speak one summer night.

"What can defeat greed, technological superiority, and legal lawlessness," Graham had finished up, "is discipline, consciousness, and unity."

Always three sentences that folks would take home for discussion, for transformation into well-ordered paragraphs that wound up, some of them, in the co-op newsletter or on the posters or in the church's bulletin. Many became primers for the children.

Graham had been wearing the denim suit with the leather

buckles the first night in class. Same fancy suit she'd caught sight of through the screen door when he'd come calling on Miz Mama Mae to buy the horse. A denim suit not country-cut at all—in fact, so *not* she was sure he would be leaving. Dudes in well-cut denim'd been coming and leaving since the days she wore but one yard of cloth. It was his would-be-moving-on clothes that had pulled her to him. But then the pull had become too strong to push against once his staying-on became clear.

She often fixed him supper in a metal cake tin once used for buttons. And Miz Mama Mae joked with the pin cushion, saying the girl weren't fooling nobody but herself sneaking around silly out there in the pantry with the button box. Telling the bobbins it was time certain folk grew up to match they size. And into the night, treadling away on the machine, the woman addressed the dress form, saying a strong, serious-type schoolteacher man had strong, serious work to do. Cutting out the paper patterns, the woman told the scissors that visiting a man in his rooms at night could mean disaster or jubilee one. And Virginia understood she would not be stopped by the woman. But some felt she was taking up too much of his time, their time. He was no longer where they could find him for homework checks or questions about the law. And Jake and Old Man Boone sullen, nervous that the midnight strategy meetings were too few now and far between. The women of the nearby district would knock and enter with trapped firefly lanterns, would shove these on the table between the couple, and make their point as Graham nodded and Virginia giggled or was silent, one.

His quilt, Graham explained, leaving the earrings on the table for her to find, was made from patches from his daddy's overalls, and scraps from Boone's wedding cutaway, white remnants from his mother's shroud, some blue from a sister's graduation, and khaki, too, snatched from the uniform he'd been proud of killing in in Korea a hundred lives ago. The day students had stitched a liberation flag in one corner. The night students had restuffed it and made a new border. She and Miz Mama Mae had stitched it and aired it. And Virginia had brought it back to him, wrapped in it. She had rolled herself all in it, to hide from him in her new earrings, childish. But he never teased that she was too big for games, and she liked that. He found her in it, his tongue finding the earrings first. Careful, girl, she'd warned herself. This could be a trap, she murmured under him.

"Be my woman," he whispered into her throat.

You don't have time for me, she didn't say, lifting his tikis and medallions up over his head. And there'd never be enough time here with so many people, so much land to work, so much to do, and the wells not even dug, she thought, draping the chains around his bedpost.

"Be my woman, Gin," he said again. And she buried her fingers in his hair and he buried his hair inside her clothes and she pulled the quilt close and closed him in, crying.

She was leaking. The earrings tinkling against her neck. The medallions clinking against the bedpost in her mind. Gray splotches stiffened in her new pink blouse, rubbing her nipples raw. But other than a dribble that oozed momentarily down her back, there was no sign of the baby aroused and hungry. If the baby slept on, she'd keep on. She wanted to reach Revun Michaels before the white men came. Came this time brazenly with the surveyors and the diggers, greedy for the granite under the earth. Wanted to catch Revun Michaels before he showed them his teeth and wouldn't hear her, couldn't, too much smiling. Wanted to hear him say it—the land's been sold. The

largest passel of land in the district, the church holdings where
the co-op school stood, where two storage sheds of the co-op
stood, where the graphics workshop stood, where four families
had lived for generations working the land. The church had
sold the land. He'd say it, she'd hear it, and it'd be over with.
She and Graham could go.

She was turning the bend now, forgetting to not look, and
the mural the co-op had painted in eye-stinging colors stopped
her. FACE UP TO WHAT'S KILLING YOU, it demanded. Below the
statement a huge triangle that from a distance was just a
triangle, but on approaching, as one muttered 'how deadly can
a triangle be?' turned into bodies on bodies. At the top, fat,
fanged beasts in smart clothes, like the ones beneath it laughing, drinking, eating, bombing, raping, shooting, lounging on
the backs of, feeding off the backs of, the folks at the base,
crushed almost flat but struggling to get up and getting up,
topple the structure. She passed it quickly. All she wanted to
think about was getting to Revun Michaels quick to hear it.
Sold the land. Then she'd be free to string together the bits
and scraps of things for so long bobbing about in her head.
Things that had to be pieced together well, with strong thread
so she'd have a whole thing to shove through the mesh at
Graham that afternoon.

And would have to shove hard or he'd want to stay, convinced that folks would battle for his release, would battle for
themselves, the children, the future, would keep on no matter
how powerful the thief, no matter how little the rain, how
exhausted the soil, 'cause this was home. Not a plot of earth
for digging in or weeping over or crawling into, but home. Near
the Ethiopic where the ancestral bones spoke their speak on
certain nights if folks stamped hard enough, sang long enough,
shouted. Home. Where "America" was sung but meant some-

thing altogether else than it had at the old school. Home in the future. The future here now developing. Home liberated soon. And the earth would recover. The rain would come. The ancient wisdoms would be revived. The energy released. Home a human place once more. The bones spoke it. The spirit spoke, too, through flesh when the women gathered at the altar, the ancient orishas still vibrant beneath the ghostly patinas some thought right to pray to, but connected in spite of themselves to the spirits under the plaster.

WE CANNOT LOSE, the wall outside the church said. She paused at the bulletin board, the call-for-meeting flyers limp in the heat. She bent to spit but couldn't raise it. She saw Revun Michaels in the schoolhouse window watching her. He'd say it. Sold the land.

Virginia wondered what the men in her ruined garden were telling themselves now about land as power and land and man tied to the future, not the past. And what would they tell the women when the bulldozers came to claim the earth, to maim it, rape it, plunder it all with that bone-deep hatred for all things natural? And what would the women tell the children dangling in the tires waiting for Jake to ring the bell? Shouting from the clubhouses built in the trees? The slashed trees oozing out money into the white man's pails, squeezing hard to prolong a tree life, forestalling the brutal cut down to stump. Then stump wasting, no more money to give, blown up out of the earth, the iron claw digging deep and merciless to rip out the taproots, leaving for the children their legacy, an open grave, gouged out by a gene-deep hatred for all things natural, for all things natural that couldn't turn a quick penny quick enough to dollar. She spit.

Revun Michaels, small and balding, was visible in the schoolhouse window. His expression carried clear out the window to her, watching her coming fast, kicking himself for getting caught in there and only one door, now that the shed was nailed on fast in back.

"Did you sell the land as well?" she heard herself saying, rushing in the doorway much too fast. "You might have waited like folks asked you. You didn't have to. Enough granite under this schoolhouse alone"—she stamped, frightening him—"to carry both the districts for years and years, if we developed it ourselves." She heard the "we ourselves" explode against her teeth and she fell back.

"Wasn't me," he stammered. "The church board saw fit to—"

"Fit!" She was advancing now, propelled by something she had no time to understand. "Wasn't nuthin fitten about it." She had snatched the ruler from its hook. The first slam hard against the chair he swerved around, fleeing. The next cracked hard against his teeth. His legs buckled under and he slid down, his face frozen in disbelief. But nothing like the disbelief that swept through her the moment "we ourselves" pushed past clenched teeth and nailed her to the place, a woman unknown. She saw the scene detached, poster figures animated: a hefty woman pursuing a scrambling man in and out among the tables and chairs in frantic games before Jake rang the bell for lessons to commence.

"And what did the white folks pay you to turn Graham in and clear the way? Disturber of the peace. What peace? Racist trying to incite a riot. Ain't that how they said it? Outside agitator, as you said. And his roots put down here long before you ever came. When you were just a twinkle in Darwin's eye." Virginia heard herself laughing. It was a good, throaty laugh and big. The man was turning round now on the floor, staring at her in amazement.

"Thirty pieces of silver, maybe? That's what you preach,

tradition. Thirty pieces 'bout as traditional as—"

"Just hold on. It wasn't me that— The board of trustees advised me that this property could not be used for—"

The ruler came down on the stiff of his arm and broke. Michaels dropped between two rickety chairs that came apart on top of him. The baby cried, the woman shushed, as much to quiet the woman that was her. Calm now, she watched the man try to get up, groping the chairs the folks had put together from cast-offs for the school. Her shoe caught him at the side of his head and he went under.

The station wagon was pulling up as she was coming out, flinging the piece of ruler into the bushes. She realized then that the men had come in it, that the station wagon had been sitting all morning in her garden. That they had come to take her to see Graham. She bit her lip. She never gave folk a chance, just like Miz Mama Mae always fussed. Never gave them or herself a chance to speak the speak.

"We'll take you to him," Jake was saying, holding the door open and easing the baby off her back.

The young one shoved over. "Mother Lee who's secretary-ing for the board has held up the papers for the sale. We came to tell you that." He waited till she smiled to laugh. "We're the delegation that's going to confront the board this evening. Us and Frankie Lee Taylor and—"

"Don't talk the woman to death," said Boone, turning in his seat and noting her daze. He was going to say more, but the motor drowned him out. Virginia hugged the baby close and unbuttoned her blouse.

"That's one sorry piece of man," drawled Boone as they pulled out. All heads swung to the right to see the short, fat, balding preacher darting in and out among the gravestones for the sanctuary of the church. To the phone, Virginia figured.

And would they jail her too, she and the baby?

Then everyone was silent before the naked breast and the sucking. Silence was what she needed. And time, to draw together tight what she'd say to Graham. How blood had spurted from Revun Michaels's ear, for one thing. Graham might not want to hear it, but there was no one else to tell it to, to explain how it was when all she thought she wanted was to hear it said flat out—land's been sold, school's no more. Not that a school's a building, she argued with herself, watching the baby, playing with the image of herself speaking her speak finally in the classroom, then realizing that she already had. By tomorrow the women would have burrowed beneath the tale of some swinging door or however Revun Michaels would choose to tell it. But would the women be able to probe and sift and explain it to her? Who could explain her to her?

And how to explain to Graham so many things. About this new growth she was experiencing, was thinking on at night wrapped in his quilt. Not like the dread growing up out of her clothes as though she'd never stop 'fore she be freak, 'cause she had stopped. And not like the new growth that was the baby, for she'd expected that, had been prepared. More like the toenail smashed the day the work brigade had stacked the stones to keep the road from splitting apart. The way the new nail pushed up against the old turning blue, against the gauze and the tape, stubborn to establish itself. A chick pecking through the shell, hard-headed and hasty and wobbly. She might talk of it this time. She was convinced she could get hold of it this time.

She recalled that last visiting time trying to speak on what was happening to her coming through the shell. But had trouble stringing her feelings about so many things together, words to drape around him, to smother all those other things, things she had said, hurled unstrung, flung out with tantrum heat at a time when she thought there would always be time enough to coolly take them back, be woman warm in some elsewhere place and make those hurtful words forgettable. But then they had come for him in the afternoon, came and got him, took him from the schoolhouse in handcuffs. And when she had visited him in the jail, leaning into the mesh, trying to push past the barrier, she could tell the way the guards hovered around her and baby that clearly they thought she could do, would do, what they had obviously tried over and over to do, till Graham was ashy and slow, his grin lax. That she could break him open so they could break him down. She almost had, not knowing it, leaking from the breast as she always did not keeping track of the time. Stuttering, whining, babbling, hanging on to the mesh with one hand, the other stuffed in her mouth, her fingers ensnarled in the skein of words coming out all tangled, knotted.

"I don't mind this so much," he'd cut in. "Time to think."

And when she pulled her fingers from her mouth, the thread broke and all her words came bouncing out in a hopeless scatter of tears and wails until something—her impatience with her own childishness, or maybe it was the obvious pleasure of the guards—made her grab herself up. She grabbed herself up abrupt, feeling in that moment what it was she wanted to say about her nights wrapped up in the quilt smelling him in it, hugging herself, grabbing herself up and trying to get to that place that was beginning to seem more of a when than a where. And the when seemed to be inside her if she could only connect.

"I kinda like the quiet," he had said. "Been a while since I've had so much time to think." And then he grinned and was ugly. Was that supposed to make her hate him? To hate and let go? That had occurred to her on the bus home. But roaming around the house, tripping on the edges of the quilt, she had rejected it. That was not the meaning of his words or that smile that had torn his face. She'd slumped in the rocking chair feeding the baby, examining her toenail for such a time.

"They never intended to dig the wells, that's clear," Old Man Boone was saying. "That was just to get into the district, get into our business, check out our strength. I was a fool," he muttered, banging his pipe against his leg remembering his hopefulness, his hospitality even. "A fool."

"Well, gaddamn, Boone," the tall gent sputtered. "Can't you read? That's what our flyers been saying all along. Don't you read the stuff we put out? Gaddamnit, Boone."

"If you don't read the flyers, you leastways knows history," the young one was saying. "When we ever invited the beast to dinner he didn't come in and swipe the napkins and start taking notes on the tablecloth 'bout how to take over the whole house?"

"Now that's the truth," Jake said, laughing. His laughter pulled Virginia forward, and she touched his arm, moved. That he could laugh. His farm stolen and he could laugh. But that was one of the three most moving things about Jake, she was thinking. The way he laughed. The way he sweated. The way he made his body comfy for the children to lean against.

"Yeh, they sat right down to table and stole the chicken," said Jake.

"And took the table. And the deed." The tall gent smacked Jake on his cap.

"Yeh," Old Man Boone muttered, thinking of Graham. "We ain't nowhere's licked yet though, huhn?"

The men looked quickly at Virginia, Jake turning clear around, so that Boone leaned over to catch the steering wheel.

"Watch it, watch it now, young feller."

"There's still Mama Mae's farm," Virginia continued, patting the baby. "Enough granite under there even if the church do—"

"But they ain't," said the young one. "Listen, we got it all figured out. We're going to bypass the robbers and deal directly with the tenant councils in the cities, and we're—"

"Don't talk the woman to death," soothed Boone. "You just tell Graham his landlady up there in the North won't have to eat dog food no more. No more in life. New day coming."

"And you tell him . . ."—Jake was turning around again— "just tell him to take his care."

By the time the bolt had lifted and she was standing by the chair, the baby fed and alert now in her arms, she had done with all the threads and bits and shards of the morning. She knew exactly what to tell him, coming through the steel door now, reaching for the baby he had not held yet, could not hold now, screened off from his father. All she wished to tell him was the bail'd been paid, her strength was back, and she sure as hell was going to keep up the garden. How else to feed the people?

THE
APPRENTICE

"Is that a brother?"

Naomi was already pulling over before I even finished hearing her question. Had pulled over and was opening her door before I spotted what had caught her attention. It was a brother all right, spread-eagle over the hump of a blue station wagon. The cop doing an excessively rough frisk. Barking out commands so gruff, his movements so baroque up through the brother's legs and over the ass, making the brother jump, then half turn, that I half suspected a set-up. A set-up or a badly done TV drama. But it was a real police car there, door ajar, squawk box intoning, topknot spinning in mesmerizing red. A too-real police car and a surreal cop.

"Hey, watch it," the brother saying, his face visible now as he was turning, the streetlight slanting down between the trees.

"Shut up and turn around." The cop had grabbed him under

the armpit and hurled him around, slamming him back up against the car hard.

"Excuse me, Officer," Naomi was saying in that voice she'd cultivated special for such occasions. "I have no intention of interfering, but I wondered if I could ask this gentlemen here if there's anyone he'd like us to call on his behalf. If that's all right . . . sir."

The cop looked over in my direction to check out her "us" business. I tried to look firm, calm and legal-like, though clearly he couldn't see me. I wondered if I should get out of the car or what. Three against one was probably on his mind. Just then Naomi stepped to the side as though to make clear she wasn't trying to block either his path to his car or his view of ours.

"You know this bum?"

When Naomi didn't answer, he looked over his shoulder at her, but did not release his man. His beefy paws still splayed out on the back, leaning against him hard, mashing his man into the car, taking him out of the action whatever it might turn out to be. Naomi took a step backward, this time I guess to let him know she wasn't thinking about going for his gun. Personally, I couldn't take my eyes off it, so very visible and takeable, and his arms way up on the brother's back.

"If this joker would get up off me so I can breathe, there's a friend . . ."

The cop dropped his arms quickly and spun away, one hand on his holster. He looked at Naomi, glanced in my direction again. In moments like this I probe beneath the layers of bluff and tough to inspect the mush that is me inside. I checked for leakage. I was doing okay. Mostly cause Naomi looked so sure, standing there, legs apart like a tree standing in the water— Naomi was not about to be moved.

"No need for that," the cop said, waving the brother's hands back on the car, in case he was planning to reach for an address book or pencil. "Just a routine check," he said to Naomi. "Got a report of a stolen car," he said to the blue station wagon. He waved again toward the hood where evidently, I couldn't see, the registration and license were. I wondered just how the scene had gone down before we arrived. And how the hell he could've checked if the papers were on the hood still and not in his possession, not in the police car. Routine, right. "Get going," he finally said, taking a Cagney stance that forced a smile out of me. Cops kill me, they really do . . . they probably will, hanging out with this Naomi person.

The brother rearranged his clothes slowly, smoothing himself, moving back into cool rhythms, leaned over and snatched something from the hood, looking good, taking his own sweet stylin time. Then nodded to Naomi and got into his car. Naomi didn't move. The cop didn't move. She watched the cop. The cop watched her. The brother cranked up and turned his wheels. They both backed out the way and the station wagon took off with squealing tires. Naomi came back briskly to the car.

"Let him go first," she said, as though I was driving and had any say-so in the matter. "He'll want to get our license plates to maybe fuck with us later. Write this down."

I scrambled into the glove compartment and banged a knee. Fit punishment, for I should've been taking notes all the while. I quickly jotted down the episode, the cop car info, the brother's plates, which Naomi rattled off, the badge number, she even had the color of the cop's eyes and a skin-mole with hair. Leave it to Naomi. The police car took off, raising a helluva lot of dust, then turned off into Maiden Lane. Naomi was making a production out of grooming herself in the rear-view mirror. To calm me down. I need a lot of soothing. Maybe by the time I get salt and pepperish in the bush like Naomi, I'll be ready for these scenes. Meanwhile, it's internal hemorrhaging for me.

"He's playing possum," Naomi said, tapping on the wheel. "Waiting for us to glide by so he can tail us."

"Whatta we do?" I asked. I was all for making a U-turn. But that wouldn't be too cool. Tried conjuring up the pack of dogs that sometimes terrorized the neighborhood in the early mornings. But at this hour they'd be clear cross town. Dogs never where you need em. Conjured em up anyway and loved the scene in Maiden Lane. German shepherds eating cop. Just about to apologize to Naomi for being so useless in a crunch when a broke-down convertible sped by, tumbled down with beer-swilling frat boys, swerving on both sides of the white line.

"Made to order," said Naomi, easing off the curb. Up ahead we saw the police car shoot out of Maiden Lane in hot pursuit of the white boys. We cracked up, turning south toward the restaurant strip.

We'd had a long, long day and I could taste coffee. I was tired, but no sense mentioning that to Naomi though. She'd come back with something like "We haven't earned the right yet to feel tired." And if I proved a hardhead and insisted my feet were burning up, she'd start ticking off the names of sisters and brothers who'd given their lives, and of course that'd cool me out. Or sometimes she'd look at me real serious and sad and not at all sarcastic like the words sounded—"And is that what you'll tell the grandchildren growing up in the detention camps, you were too tired to seize state power?" She'd hug me even. Cept she's tall and skinny, so her hugs're very much like a headlock, if I'm feeling paranoid. "Too tired even to get information out, to try to hook up folk, or work a little for the people?" There's no talking to the woman.

Naomi assumes everybody wakes up each morning plotting out exactly what to do to hasten the revolution. If you mention to her, for example, that you are working on a project or thinking about going somewhere or buying something, she'll listen enthusiastically waiting for you to get to the point, certain that it will soon all be revealed if she is patient. Then you finish saying what you had to say, and she shrugs—"But how does that free the people?" And you wind up jumping up and down screaming about yeah, yeah that was the most important question but dammit not the only one. If you weren't careful you'd find yourself spinning out one of those farmer-in-the-dell numbers: I want to buy these boots, you see; boss boots allow me to walk; walking I meet the people; I am cheerful with the people cause I'm in my boots, you see. And so forth and so forth in the house that Jack built. But for all my hollerin, I love the sister and am always refreshed, coming off work, to see her car idling at the curb, ready to make the rounds, keep this committee in touch with that project in touch with thusnsuch organization in touch with the whatchmacallit league.

Early this afternoon Naomi had picked me up at the print shop where I slave from seven to three-thirty with time off for good behavior to pee and to eat. The sweatshop where I do my time burning up brain cells printing rah-rah pamphlets for the chamber of commerce or gosh almighty brochures for the motels. Today I at least got a chance to run off the flyers we need for the food rally, so I felt ahead of the game. Felt good seeing her at the curb cause we'd start our rounds at the senior citizen complex. Love me some wise old jovial elders. Though quite frankly, a visit to the morgue would be a pleasure after being holed up in the airless, noisy joint all day moving greasy type around.

Naomi always goes upstairs to the old folks' lounge to mess around on the piano and fill up the bulletin board with clippings and flyers. Music always draws a crowd and provides an occasion for rappin. And Naomi is a big-league rapper on the corner, in the church, wherever. I'm mostly a listener. So I like the downstairs laundry room. There was a bunch of women in the basement this afternoon, magazines idle on their laps, talking in drifts about food stamps and literacy classes and who did or didn't get rent receipts back yet. I eased on in during the breaks in the drift, greeted everybody, took a turn at commenting on the importance of keeping fit. The littlest one of the old mamas did most of the talking. I liked the way she glided into every statement with a "Weeelll." When the drift got real blurry, I cleared my throat and was fixin to ask them if they supported the Right to Eat Food Co-op's demands and were they coming to the rally. But that ain't no way to come at people, head-on and blunt. I been studying the way Naomi do it and am always amazed at all this patience she got stored up, cause she ain't always patient with me, Lord knows.

"You look like a woman who knows her Bible," I said to Little Weeelll.

"Weeelll," she said, adjusting her buns on the lopsided folding chair, "the Good Book has taught me to live right and resist wrong. And I'm a living, fighting eighty-four today and here to tell it." We were off and running. Had me a good ole time with the elder ladies, badmouthed the *Senior Citizen Tribune* for habitually overlooking their center and its activities, joked about the younger generation clomping about in their Frankenstein shoes, got sober about prices in general, food in particular and the mysterious doings behind the closing of so many supermarkets in our neighborhood. That led us right into the rally the Right to Eat Food Co-op was holding next week. While they were assuring me that of course the old folks would turn out for the likes of that, I got up and made the call to City Hall, to send the Golden Age Bus Sunday week to haul folks to the rally. We hugged goodbye and agreed to fry up some chicken for our reunion in the park.

Naomi was waiting for me in the parking lot, handing out

flyers to the old folks coming to the center for craft class, but mostly talking to this old fellah leaning on a cane. Cane more for show it turned out, cause he did everything else after that one second but lean on it. Jabbed it in the dirt to make his point, tapped Naomi on the leg to get her attention when she got caught up with leafleting, smacked it against his own leg when he laughed, which was a lot. Cracked me up.

"It's just like the church," he was saying as I came up, highstepping over the uncut grass. Naomi giving him her undivided attention. "Sermon's only as good as the congregation make it. Preacher can't do much lessen you give him some encouragement, lend him your energy, your fire. Let him know you with him. Specially my preacher, who's old and can't half see. Got to shout a little, hum a little, sing, stomp, pray out loud. Get them fans going and rustle up a wind so he know you there. Ain't that right?"

"That's right," I said, prepared to shout if he called on me again.

"The man got to know his words are speaking to your life," he said, banging his cane on the already broken asphalt. "Like when I was young and had me a good voice, I sang in the choir," he continued, bouncing gingerly from the knees to show us he had some spring left. "I'd fill in the empty music spaces asking, 'Am I spoilin ya? Am I spoilin ya?' Remember how folks used to do that?"

"Yessir," I said, getting the hang of it. "And you'd be spoilin them, I bet."

"Course I was. Sure. And they'd answer me, join in the singing, raise they voice, shout 'Amen!' You got to let the people in, ya see. They got to be a part of the whole musical thing or whatever's the program."

Naomi and I nodded vigorously while he puffed a bit at the thoroughly cold cigar, gazing out over the terrain—the senior citizen apartment house, the community center, the school-yard, the bus stop, the rickety houses across the boulevard.

"Take this community, for example," he said. "Many people here still movin on, fightin for rights, scufflin to keep goin. But they got to tarry a while and ask us old folks, 'Am I spoilin ya?' And we got to answer, say amen, take part in the thing. You understand what I'm saying?"

"It's the truth," I said.

"So I just wanna thank yawl for coming by here and sharing of your time, letting us know what's going on, liftin our spirits this day. See you Sunday week," he said, tucking the cigar way back in his jaw. He tipped his cap and made his way back through the high grass, his cane bobbing up and down more beating out a cadence than supporting his weight.

Naomi waved when he turned at the door, then handed me the notes. We'd be stopping at the newspapers, demanding coverage of the senior citizen contingent at the food rally. I organized the notes on the clipboard while she drove. Then I copied over neatly the poem Mother Weeelll had composed on the spot. "Good Book taught me how to live right and resist wrong," it began. "Old folks forced to eat dog food to live is as wrong as you can get," the other women had contributed. She worked that into the poem too. I figured it'd make a good companion piece to the article about the old folks and the rally.

Our third stop was Edward Decker, head of the Brothers of Canaan Lodge. I tried to talk Naomi into letting me go straight on to the tenant's council and meet her later at the public housing hearing. Naomi gave me a look. Decker welcomed our visit warmly enough and assured us his lodge supported the rally. But then he hauled out the scrapbooks, gave us a tour of the house, made long speeches about the framed citations on the living room walls and was the general drag I'd always found him to be. So bitter cause, according to him, Black folks had spoiled his triumph for him. Just would not acknowledge the man as a leader, a man who'd given so unselfishly, he told us, of his talents, his time, his energy.

"All this talk about Black mayors," he snorted, serving half cups of coffee and paper-thin cake. "I could've been mayor, but colored folks were backward then, jealous of anyone who had an education and wanted to get ahead."

"Busing?" he asked, eyes wide, looking around as though someone hiding had just challenged him on the issue. "I was fighting for integrated schools long before all this busing fuss. Sent my own boys to the Sacred Heart Academy in Rosedale. Cost me a pretty penny too. First coloreds there. You think my people appreciated what I was trying to do?" He slammed the bulging scrapbook shut. *"Ebony* didn't even have the courtesy to answer my letter. And there I was providing a good example for colored people who wanted to get along, who wanted to get ahead."

"Did you know," he asked, whisking away our rations before we'd touched them, "I was the first colored admitted to the American Legion here? And the first colored in this district to start a Liberty Bond drive—in '42, it was?"

"And the first live mascot of the KKK," I mumbled, him clear out of earshot in the kitchen mostly talking to himself.

Naomi gave me a look. I knew what it meant. Cynicism, sarcasm, smugness was defeatist, benefited nobody but the enemy, that look said. The job is to develop the progressive forces, win over the indifferent, and isolate the diehards, that look said. And the diehard was not just any ole body I didn't like, as the group instructed me at last criticism session, or folks I hastily bumped off out of a reluctance to work. A diehard is one energetically working to disrupt unity, fighting against health and sanity, delaying willfully the liberation of the people. My work attitude ain't too progressive, I've been told more than once at the group criticism sessions. I am negative. I guess that's why I've been teamed with Naomi. She views everything and everybody as potentially good, as a possible hastener of the moment, an usherer in of the new day. Examines everybody in terms of their input to making revolution an irresistible certainty.

Easy for Naomi—hell, she'd been to countries where ordinary folk had done it, had stood up and flexed their knees, and in that simple gesture toppled the whole johnson built on their backs, feeding off their backs, breaking their backs for generations after generation. What have I seen but junkies noddin in the alley, dudes steppin in my window to rip me off, folks that'd kill God for a quarter. Easy for Naomi, she's been to countries where dirt farmers and factory workers had broken the hold of the greedy on the people, seized power and turned the whole thing around. Built schools and hospitals for their neighbors, themselves. Distributed the food, the health, the wealth with equity—first to the ones who needed it most, the ones so miserably shortchanged for years. Hell, what do I know about people like that. They tell me at the criticism sessions that I do so know people like that but refuse to remember, refuse to recognize, cause recognition commits me to work. Shit, I'm working, ain't I? Submit to criticism, don't I? What do they want from me?

I use to tell my mama—being somebody can sure be hard on a person, meaning mostly my elbows and my behind and my ears sitting up in school all day long and church all night long and on my knees at bedtime and in Grandma's kitchen listening to her over the oatmeal and listening to Daddy and Granddaddy talk my ears off as they drove me to school in the pick-up. Being a revolutionary is something else again. I'm not sure I'm up to it, and that's the truth. I'm too little, and too young, and maybe too scarified if you want to know the truth.

33

It's just a matter of time, time and work, Naomi always saying, cause the revolution is here. No sense asking where, though, you get a look. I could see it maybe if she said it was just around the corner. Then I could ask her to lighten up a bit. It's hard on me, this work. They gave me a whole school district to profile and organize by winter. Ain't hardly autumn and already I'm falling apart. Them junior high kids burn me out. Just now coming to understand how come intermediate schools are necessary, why they got to build a special place for just them two or three years—cause them kids are crazy, that's why. Show me a thirteen-year-old, I'll show you a menace, a monster, a nut. Crazy, loud, ignorant and dangerous. Yeah, yeah, I'm trying to change and not be so negative. But damn, them kids is hard on my nerves, not to mention my feet.

"Where all this crowd coming from?" Naomi asking, rescuing me from my cataloguing of the day's rounds.

Traffic look more like nine in the morning than eleven at night. Even the side streets're jammed with buses and cars and kids walking five abreast in the streets. We turn off slowly toward Larry's Diner. I'm glad of that, starving to death and needing a bathroom, and tasting that coffee slick on my teeth.

"Come the revolution," I say, "we'll set up public toilets and you won't need a dime neither. That way old folks'll feel more like getting about, won't be frettin about their bladders. And kids won't have to try to make it to the fifteenth floor of the projects, ruining their health." Not to mention the elevators, I do not say. I get to wondering, though, if there'll be projects after the revolution. Once land's put to proper use and not hoarded by the fatsos, won't there be space enough without folks living all on top of each other? Or maybe the projects'll be owned by the tenants and therefore better, cause people who live there would just go ahead and put toilets on the first

34

floor so the elevators would be cool. But then . . . I rub my eyeballs, so dry they clicking. Sore all over from sitting too much. The old folks, Decker's, the tenant's meeting, the public housing hearing, fifty-leven visits. We'd really covered some ground. Nothing but a small stack of flyers left about the rally. It'd been a long, long day.

"Will you just look at this," Naomi's saying. Cars jammed into all three lots of Larry's drive-in. The waiters and waitresses dressed like drum majorettes, skating from car to window to car, grabbing trays, spiking orders on the spindle, rattling the door to get relief, banging on the window to rush the order boys inside, giving lip to the loudmouths, taking shit from the surly, popping sweat in sprays visible even from where we're parked, three layers back.

"Damn. Must be a combination of the Al Green concert and the movie crowd," I say, hoping Naomi won't get it in her head to start leafleting or nothing like that. Folks hongry, hollering out the window, leaning on their horns, even when joking can be mean. I am not for getting out there trying to engage nobody in some cogent discussion about the rally and how we need to push for land reform and alternative food marketing. Not me. No way. Uhn-uhhhn.

"What was playing tonight?" Naomi asks.

I'm studying her face for a clue so I can head her off at the pass. I'm too tired for anything but eating. I answer cautiously. *Buck and the Preacher* and another rerun over at the Regent. *Cooley High* and a talent show at the Y. Some cops and robbers at the Dorset."

Then she don't say nothing. Pulls up the emergency brake and grabs the clipboard out my lap. I stay alert, ready to veto any fool notion about stepping out on the hood with a bullhorn getting up a discussion about movies or something, or how we have to control Black images and stuff like that.

"What's on your mind?" I decide to ask when I can stand it no longer.

"I was just thinking," she says slowly, writing and me trying not to get anxious, "that the Regent's a good place to run *La Luta Continua.* Only house that does a double bill. Folks might not turn out for just a film about the Mozambiquan liberation forces, but I doubt they'd walk out on it on a double bill. What do you think?"

I nod instead of speaking. Don't want to commit myself to anything less it's a fish sandwich and a cup of coffee. All she do is nod and continue writing. There's just no predicting Naomi sometime. I ease down in the seat, too tired to even go to the bathroom. It would surely be a while before we got served.

I could hear Naomi scratching away on that clipboard as I drifted off. My feet fell asleep first. I was in a good mood now —now that we were finished. I could even forgive ole stingy Decker for that coffee we never did get a chance to grab hold of. Was thinking bout how Naomi don't never let up, always teaching. At the hearing, for example, she suddenly just got up with no warning—less you want to count a mumble and some heavy teeth sucking—and strolled up to the table in front where the legislators and the housing authority biggies sitting, pours herself a glass of water. Then she pours some more, taking the mayor's glass even, and puts them on her clipboard and proceeds to serve the folks. And in that one gesture she makes us all aware that them folks at the table are sitting two feet higher than we are, got all the ashtrays, got two pitchers of ice water, and we ain't got shit. Meeting completely changed up after that. Naomi something.

"Let's hang around," Naomi is saying when I wake up and reach for my sandwich. "Let's wait till the crowd pulls out and go back to the kitchen to applaud the folk. They worked like champs. I counted eighty-seven cars in the past hour. They must be delirious back there."

Damn. I could just see ole Larry having to get out of his threads to pitch in. Hanging his jacket out back less it become a mass of grease. Rolling up his sleeves and stashing his rings in an ice bag for safekeeping. Opening crates and punching holes in catsup cans. Racing back and forth to check his coat out there, the hot fat popping, the old dude on the sandwich board making a blur of that cleaver getting to the onions, Mama Mildred working her magic on the fish and stuff, her daughter keeping that grill packed with them square hamburgers and foot-long hot dogs. Eighty-seven cars per hour! That gotta mean twenty gallons of cola syrup, two crates of tomatoes, a gross of onions, a bushel or three of them French fry somethings, seventy pounds of hamburger, forty pounds of fish, a crate of napkins and stuff, one wrenched spine, eight pairs of fallen arches, at least one sprained ankle, six pairs of worn-out ball bearings . . .

"Funny," Naomi says suddenly, shoveling onions and peppers into her mouth. "I mean you work all day, right? Dead on your feet and can't go on. But then a situation develops and you rise to the occasion, get your legs back, get your second wind. It's fantastic!" She bit off a hunk and looked so happy.

"Can you just imagine," she continued, eyes shining, "the energy that would be released if we were working for ourselves, for our neighbors, our children? If we owned the country? The whole damn country, I'm talking about. If it was ours to administer, to develop, ours?" She was hunching me, making me lose hold of my fish.

"Giiiirl, it would be too much, too much. The energy, the creativity, the humanness, the—" Then ole Naomi like to push me off balance and I can't get hold of that sucker for nothing, all I got's a mouthful of hot sauce.

"Holy shit! I mean, like suppose the workers ran the shop where you work? Imagine all the great work you'd produce. No resentment of authority. Hell, we'd be the authority. You, friends, neighbors, working people. Man, we'd work our asses off. It'd be beautiful. Beautiful. Do you hear what I'm saying? Beauuu tiii fuulll!"

I hollered right along with her, cause I could feel the energy coming back to my feet, waking up my legs. Yeah, I could feel it. Own the country? Shit, if I just owned the house I'm living in, I'd have the energy to run all the way home and plow up the yard front, side and back and plant me a garden. Grow me some butter beans and greens and squash and whatnot. Have me a stand on the highway and help fund the nursery.

"Oh, Lawd, let it come in our lifetime," Naomi shouting just like in church. Stomping on the floor mat, giving the steering wheel a thumping smack. And I bet she's thinking about that time in Cuba when she spent two whole days, or tried to, with this sister who was director of mental health, chairman of the journalism department, did voluntary labor on a construction brigade, had two kids and an invalid father, and liked to party ole Naomi to death in the all-night outdoor dance halls. And I just bet she was thinking bout them folks in the Sea Islands who organized against the golf-course developers and even got the Arabs to put up some money in front to beat out the Jew landbarons. Organized their farms collectively, built a school and trained some organizers, sent some folk to law school and still moving, plus like to party ole Naomi in the ground to boot.

"Whoooweee," Naomi shouting, wailing on the steering wheel and thinking about God knows who else. I'm about to point out that this is the first time I've ever seen her just go right off. But she's raising such a ruckus she can't even hear me. Plus I'm kinda caught up in the thing myself. I can feel the new day Naomi always lecturing about, can feel it pumping through my legs. I want to be there. I'm hoping I live long enough. I'm just about to make some promises to work harder when one of the waitresses rolls up and takes hold to our tray.

"You all were fantastic," says Naomi, and we both applaud the sister real loud. She looks stunned. "I know you beat, sister, and if you ain't got a lift we'd be honored to drive you. Yawl worked and then some."

"That's the truth," the sister say, panting, hanging on the door handle, breathless, wet, about to just give it up and fall out. "Got a lift, but hey, thanks." She ghosts a smile and pushes off from the car, reeling, stumbling, careening into a brother with trays piled high, looking like a circus act. I cover my eyes, can't bear to look. Naomi taps me on my arm to say it was only a near disaster.

Ain't but about six cars left. And already the drum majorettes're yanking off the helmets and rolling toward the back, unbuttoning the uniforms, leaning on each other, stumbling against the windows. Me and Naomi go through the side door toward the kitchen. But before we even get there we choking and gagging. Grease so thick it gets up under your tongue, coats your teeth, feel like blobs of it in my ear cause I can't half hear Mama Mildred calling hello. The hot metal stench did something to the lining of my throat and I can't answer right away, the scorch like still-burning cinders. Onion juice in the air bringing stinging tears to the eyes. My face downright juicy.

Mama Mildred leaning up in the counter window, her elbow anchoring her heft, jerking in spasms, her apron a mess of catsup and hot sauce. They all look like some medico team just in from the front. Her daughter having a giggling fit over the grill, bearing down hard on the wire brush with both hands, I thought the giggling would land her face down on that steamy grill.

"That was some crowd, hunh?" Larry leaning up against the refrigerator, sucking on a sliver of ice. "Great God Almighty, that was some bunch of people come through her, hunh?" I thought he was about to break into a tap dance, but realize he just trying to untangle them crate cords from his cuffs. A square of hamburger paper stuck on a shoe and he trying to jiggle that off too.

"Well, yawl sure did it," I say, hoping they won't get it in their minds to reenact the whole johnson for us, they can barely stay on their feet or stay still for a second. "Know yawl was doing it back here. Doing it to death."

"We surely was," say Mama Mildred, swiping at the counter with her rag, distracted. "Took care plenty business back here. Plenty business."

Naomi goes on through the swinging doors and squeezes out a rag in the sink and commences to clean. I prefer to talk through the counter window, sharing the ledge with Mama Mildred's elbow. Hell, it's slippery in there. Must be a truck load of salt strewn all over the floor in there to give traction. But it ain't doing nothing but looking like day-old slush. The old dude slipping and sliding in it, trying to stack up the boxes and crates by the back door, shaking his head.

"It's a real test of character," he saying, breaking down the boxes. "Separates the amateur from the pro."

Larry skids over to him and feints a punch and a hook, then socks him lightly in the arm. "Well, you a pro, old fella, that's for sure."

"That's exactly what I was just saying." He winks. "And this guy"—thumbing at Larry—"this fool back here about to lose his mind hollerin about 'Don't panic. Don't panic.'

And he the only one panicking. Shooot. I knew we had it covered. Me and Mama Mildred has handled some crowds make this one look like early-morning shopping ladies in for coffee. Shoot."

Larry had to laugh at himself, banging around on the refrigerator, still looking for his legs. He could afford to laugh, Mama Mildred's face says, he's making the money.

"Yeah, we seen some crowds," Mama Mildred talking dreamily. "Seen some crowds in our time."

"Tell it." I couldn't help it. I am congenitally unable to pass up a story cue. "I know yawl must have handled some hongry people through the years."

"I tell you this," the old gent begins, collapsin down on the stacks of broken boxes, "I was once a Peace man, worked for Father Divine and the people. We used to feed umpteen folks around the clock. Am I lyin?"

"Naaw," say Mama Mildred, coming to life. "Poor people from all over the city would tote their families into Father's restaurants. Salisbury steak, pickled beets, macaroni and cheese, iced tea and milk for thirty-five cents."

"Sometimes twenty-five. Ain't that right? Twenty-five. And don't forget the pound cake and Jello, Millie. I'd come in there after work expecting to put in my four hours and get on home to my room. Had a room in Miss Hazel's place in those days, remember?"

"I remember. Yeh, you'd sho nuff do the shift you came to do. But, honey, when them peoples start to come in there, wasn't bout no shifts. Like at Thanksgiving or Christmas. Mercy! Them was some times."

"Yeh, some times. But hell, poor people always got to be fed," the old gent talking. "You can say what you want about the Depression and them soup lines, but colored folks always on some soup line or other. And always will be, I guess."

"Naaw," say Naomi, wiping down the refrigerator, and moving Larry out the way to do it. "Not always, Pop Feather. You know good and well that ain't the truth. We got a brighter future than that."

"I hear you," he says, staring off into space as though he could see it too. "One day I'm gonna have me a gumbo joint in Galveston. Gonna keep a folk-price menu too. Feed me some folks."

"Count me in," say Mama Mildred, lifting her elbow from the counter to raise her hand. "When it come to feeding the people, you know I'm ready."

I hang in the window and watch them work. The giggling teen-ager off the grill now and changing bulbs. Larry and the ole gent dragging boxes out. Mama Mildred wiping off the counter window, wiping around me. Naomi scrubbing and mopping and sweeping and carrying on like she getting time and a half for overtime. I am there for the stories myself. It seems to refresh them and that's cool, I figure I'm doing my part keeping the folks going. The last of the waiters in mufti hands me the keys and I'm wishing I had me a pair of them skates, cause I can't see how I'm going to make it back to the car, I'm so beat. No use saying nothing to Naomi, though, bout being tired. I ain't earned the right, to hear her tell it. But hell, it'd been a long, long, long day.

Broken
Field
Running

Jason and I stop for the third time trying to talk to each other, the wind blowing our words away fast as we shout them out. Folks bent over and squinting in the snow duck between us, knocking us off balance. But we decide somehow, clutching at each other's lapels, to not split the group in two mainly cause we want to stay together. Besides, the kids have come to expect that—Dada Lacey and Ndugu Jason, together in school and out, their teachers, their responsibles, friends.

"Come on, Dada Lacey." The children calling and racing ahead. Malaika doing a one-hand cartwheel right smack in the middle of rush-hour folks. Teenagers bounding from the buses all scarfed up like Jesse James. Workers bustling, scrambling over the banks of dirty snow serious about the business of getting home.

"Careful," Jason's shouting to the kids, but the wind shoves the word down his throat and only I hear it, my face damn near buried in his woolly arm and still can't see a blessed thing. My world a maze of brown-green plaid one minute, snow the next. I'm trusting Jason to count the hoods, caps, pompoms as the kids scoot into the alley taking the shortcut to the Lawndale projects. I'm feeling out of it.

The Hawk and his whole family doing their number on Hough Avenue, rattling the panes in the poolroom window, brushing up bald spots on the cat from the laundry poised, shaking powder from his paw, stunned. Ain't snowed in these parts for years and years. The Christmas bells on the pole outside the Black Pig Bar-b-que whipping around but hanging on by the cord. Flicking my lashes I can see where I'm going for about a minute till the wind gusts up again, sweeping all up under folks' clothes doing a merciless sodomy. Wind lashing the back of my coat apart where the vent I once thought was so fly is. I make a note to sew that sucker up first chance I get.

"Ain't this a bitch!" I holler in Jason's ear. "Roughed off by Jack Frost in broad daylight."

"What daylight?" Jason hollers back.

"Come on," Kwane's urging, standing dead in the middle of the alley much as we've told the kids about staying alert for pint bottles pitched from the Black Pig or garbage dumped from above. The kid glances up at a fat woman in a frayed bathrobe adjusting the window shade over the laundry, then runs on, the lesson only now reaching his "remind," as he says.

There's a flurry of snow masking the projects, as though the enemy's ordered a whiteout in our part of town. For a minute the Lawndale Homes is a snow-scene paperweight some kid's been shaking. Then the sound of the kids whooping and hollering across the open area reaches us and the scene is what it is again—free-flowing terrain designed to leave the issue of territorial control up for grabs.

Hawk and his Mama've commandeered no man's land between the sidewalk and the garbage bins to the left of the building. Drug dealers got squatter's rights where a bench should be but ain't, so there's no Pop Johnson and checker cronies to assert jurisdiction over the space. Take-off artists and bullies of one sort or another slink about in the zones where a stoop should be but ain't, where Apartment 1A's window for surveying all comings and goings should be but ain't. The missing observation posts for defining space and defending turf creating a deliberate vacuum. And vipers will rush in where tenants fear to tread.

"I'd like to meet the characters that designed these places," I'm growling, "in an alley . . . with my chisel."

Jason yanks me out of the path of oil cans tumbling from out of nowhere. Together we hop an Octagon soap box banging around trying to get traction. I can't believe I'm seeing broken whiskey bottles all over, on top of the snow. It's doing something to me inside.

"Come on, slowpokes," the kids holler, trying to open the heavy door to the building. They didn't have kids in mind when they put the place together. But then they didn't have people in mind from the jump. Some wrong-looking characters are lurking in the outer lobby, ringing bells, unscrewing the lobby bulbs, and not opening the door for the kids.

Bene comes skidding into me like he's on a skateboard. "Hurry up. I gotta pee."

We grab him by the arms and race to the door. Of course the kid lives on the twelfth floor. And quite naturally the designers of Lawndale have not installed a bathroom on the ground floor for such bizarre occasions as this. And there's no bathroom in the play area either, cause there is no play area for the sixty families averaging three kids apiece. So the elevator got to do triple duty.

"Yeahhh," I'm mumbling, burnt toast and lard jamming up

my sensors the minute I hit the door, "I'd like to study the
brains of these planners up close, Jason. Forceps in hand."

"Lacey," Jason's heaving against the big door, giving me
another tired look. "The trick is to be selective. Gotta side-step
some of the shit. Can't just go off behind everything, Lacey.
Gotta keep stepping."

The dudes checking out which apartments ain't buzzing
back don't even turn around. The kids swarm in past Jason's
legs and start singing just to hear themselves now that there's
no wind to bend and blow their sounds about. The bell ringers
glance around, frowning at the kids, then spy Jason and decide
to take a walk. I study Jason for a minute, wondering what sort
of look he gave them, then decide it's just Jason, all that he is.
If you a wrong type, you automatically take a walk. They don't
take much of a walk, though. Just outside by the bushes planted
special for rapists and muggers to leap at you from.

The buzzer is buzzing and several voices are gargling on the
intercom. Kwame and Malaika say hello and pronounce their
names real nice in response, like that'll get it. We go in the
lobby door and a blast of heat gets past the damp and frost to
chap my face. Then it goes straight for the eyes. Enemy fur-
naces to strip the mucous membranes and leave us vulnerable
to the viruses cultivated special in the prisons on the rest of our
population.

"Lacey?"

"What?"

"You're growling again," Jason cautions.

Mommy Barbara's by the elevator with her arms crossed
over her chest like she carrying a piece up under her sweater.
She motions us to go on. Daddy Jordan comes out of 1B with
his right hand bunched up under his shirt looking in twelve
directions at once, and he too jerks his head toward the outer
door to say go on. The kids, meanwhile, are snuggling all up

into Mommy Barbara's warmth, yanking on her pockets, shouting over each other's heads, eager to relate what they'd seen and done at the African art exhibit. Smiling and trying to hear them all and not show her own Kwame any favoritism, she gets backed into the elevator and jammed up against the buttons imprinting on the back of her head.

"How the hell they expect kids to reach buttons up that high?"

"Lacey, shut up." Jason jerks me toward the door. "And yes, I know, they both had heat. Let's go."

We duck out into the dark now. I try to ignore the rape bushes, the shadows stretching and shrinking off to the side, the broken glass, the strident siren of the fire truck turning out of the alley skidding out of control, heading our way, bumping the curb, then backing up and gone. The kids, not sure which route we'll take for the next drop-off, are doing base slides in the path, cold as it is. Folks coming on fast, bearing down and looking not at all kindly like they might in summer about a bunch of kids between the Hawk and home.

"Where are the snows of yesteryear?" I'm chanting as we break into a trot. I'm really wondering where are the Pop Johnsons of my day. The elders who declared our community a sovereign place. Could raise an army and navy, draw up a peace treaty, levy taxes, declare war, settle disputes. And no sign of the the Royal Stompers, the Imperial Ten, the Hough Avenue Lords. Who establishes borders and guards frontiers now? And where are the Miss Gladyses leaning out the windows on them damn fringe pillows from the year one? The leaning newspapers, broadcasters, social arbiters, heavy-duty mothers for everyone under twenty-five. Where are the mamas heaving sighs and calling, calling? Their hurry-up voices scaling roofs and piercing handball walls and cellar stairs. The daddies with the I-tole-you-boy belts stalking hardheads in the middle of the street, Lucky Strikes jammed in the back of the jaw. The old folks in the shadows of the china closet appealing to your do-right nature.

The prodigals come home to what now? Return from the sojourn with the dead, armed with medals, sheepskin or whatever kind of dance with the dead it was. Come home to families for a transfusion. But families now are mere cargo cults. Cars, clothes, color TV, eight-track deck, lawn mowers the size of Model Ts. And whatcha bring us, boy? How much they offering, girl? A ghostly lot from college, jail, or Vietnam home for a transfusion, the prodigals are sucked dry or run over by the gold-rush stampede. My brother Buster in his old room behind locked doors, a specter sometimes seen in the hallway when I visit, casts no shade on the walls, leaves no prints in the carpet.

"Ohh lawd, where are we headed, Jason?" I'm moaning, knowing there's no refuge in the present or in the highly selective fiction I've made of the past. I'm clowning around but bleeding.

"Lenox Lake Apartments," he answers, and that will have to suffice.

Once again we're trotting along Hough Avenue, Jason doing a shonuff Jim Brown, me doing a lot of unstylish slipping and sliding in my new boots. Malaika, Abdul, and the Taylor boys zigzagging along, heads up eating snowflakes, bumping into folks and hollering "Scuse me" over their shoulders.

"If only I could fly," I'm moaning.

"I can't tell if you doing one of your numbers or got frostbite of the brain, Lacey. You're not yourself today."

"Kindly tell a dying old lady how it's going to be in the new day, Doc. Tell me how we're gonna moove and take controoool of this bad boy and turn it into a proud nation."

"Lacey, lighten up," Jason grunts, as close a laugh as he can manage with the wind right in his mouth. He throws an arm around my shoulders and hugs me close as we swing around four police cars parked square in the center of the sidewalk, blocking the entrance to the mosque. Jason slows me down to a marking-time trot.

"What's going on?" young Vincent whispers, racing back and tugging on Jason's coat.

"It's cool," two Muslim brothers in the doorway say, stepping aside so we can see the Fruit gathered in the lobby. "It's cool."

Jason stomps the snow from his boots, and we move on till we bump into the rest of the kids waiting at the curb. A hog is in the crosswalk and we can't see around to move. Three ladies flouncing up to the rolled-down window, surrendering up bills from between their tits. The pimp evil bout the cold coming in, snow flaking on his bright red upholstery.

"Hurry up, bitch." He scowls.

"Well damn, T.J.," one whines, trying to reassemble her clothes.

"Ain't she cold?" Roger asks his big brother Vincent. "She gonna catch a cold for sure."

"Steady now, Lacey," Jason croons in my ear. "In our lifetime."

We all grab hands and scoot across the street, Abdul slipping on the sewer cover nearly bringing us all down.

"Options for everybody, Lacey. And in our time."

"Promise?"

"Hell. It's a certainty."

I turn, looking over my shoulder at the skin of ice on the sewer cover, remembering the time some old lady took a spill right in front of a bus one rainy day. People moving so fast, two of us had to fight to get to her in time. The bro with the hot goods moving fast and blocking our way. The three teen-agers five layers fat in boosted clothes scurrying past. The sister rushing from work to beat the welfare lady to her door damn near knocking us over. So many forced for so long into something or other and can't afford no trouble, no encounters with cops, can't afford to make a human response.

"Whatcha doin?" Malaika is asking me, holding on to my belt and walking backwards in front of me.

"Thinking." I jut my chin in the direction of the condemned houses occupied still, faded blankets hanging in the windows, snow sifting into the hallway through the half-there door. I swing my whole head in the direction of the cathedral, its flying buttresses taking in on one side the PAL center and the bank under its wing. Shoving a tenement off its axis on the other side.

"Remind me to discuss visual gags, next time we're out walking," I say. She nods, rattling my belt to call my attention to the fact that she wants to say something that needs checking. Her lips are glazed.

"There's poor people cause there's rich people," she says and waits for a nod. "And there's rich people cause they steal from the poor, right?" She too swivels her head around and juts her chin in the direction of the cathedral and the condemned homes. "I just figured that out."

I nod sagely, trying not to step on the little red boots scurrying just in front of mine.

"What kind of people would there be if there was no rich and no poor?" Jason shouts so they can all hear and pick up the thread we dropped at the art exhibit. Equity in the new state.

"Free," Malaika says, cocking her head to the side and frowning as though Jason's some new brand of fool. "Everybody knows that."

"Do you realize, Lacey," Jason says in my ear when the kids shoot ahead toward the park, "that Western civilization is already the past for most of the Third World? We've got to prepare the children faster. Time's running out." Jason chews on his mustache that flakes. "I mean, a whole new era is borning and here we are trudging along Hough Avenue like fossils." Jason's voice crackles with impatience for the future. I long for one glimpse, one moment's respite from shit, a long beat between blues notes.

I bury my face in his sleeve again and take notes to feed him back later. Jason never got sense enough to talk into a tape recorder and preserve ideas that can blossom into lessons for the school. And each time it's his turn to do a workshop for the parents and teachers, he's got to call me for ideas, his own ideas.

"We all in this country are like the last hunters of the hunter age, seeing the first farmer come down the pike and set up a cabin."

I don't know what Jason sees, but I see ole Cain in a leopard-skin jumpsuit checking out the red neck and dirty fingernails of potato-digging, overalled Abel. Cain, hellbent on extending the feral epoch just a wee bit longer, picking up a large rock and saying, "Hey, fella, come here a minute. Could I interest you in a deer steak, or are you one of them hippie, commie vegetarian homos?"

"Can you imagine, Lacey, what it must've been like when the dude rolled out the first wheel and sent it spinning down the block? It's a whole new era coming, Lacey. All over the world. A new age." Jason's sounding solemn, awe-struck.

I stumble along, wondering whether Piltdown Pete felt dumb enough standing there on the corner holding some square thing to slay the wheeler.

"I hope I got heat in my place, cause I need to write a long time tonight," Jason says. I'm cozy at the thought of Jason's fireplace. My tongue already burned on marshmallows and runny rummed bananas crinkly with bits of tinfoil. I'm in no shape to go home alone.

The Gothic cathedral looms over us now, its tracery window an insistent eye, the gargoyles peering down on the children.

"The beggars of medieval Europe used to maim their children," I blurt out. "For economic survival. An arm here, a leg there, an eye."

Jason doesn't answer. He glances up at the cathedral, then down to some social-service agency that's sprung up when we weren't looking. It's snug between the bank and the PAL center. He takes in the stripped-down van abandoned outside, at the frosted trash piles and car shells in front of the tenement. He's making some kind of notes, composing another "Wasteland," I suspect.

We blind our children, I'm thinking. Blind them to their potential, the human potential. Cripple them, dispirit them. Cripples make good clients, wards, beggars, victims.

"An eyeless, boneless, chickenless egg. Ohhh, you'll have to be put out with a bowl to beg—"

"Lacey."

"—Children, I hardly knew yeeeww."

"Lacey. Be cool now. Don't fly off on me now. We got kids to deliver home safely."

"I need to fly. I feel like I'm being sucked down by quicksand. Do you remember the elders on Dada Swan's porch that time?"

Jason's not listening. One eye on the traffic, the other on the kids, he checks his watch and yanks me along.

The school started out eight years ago as a nursery in Swan Sanderson's house, which was fine with me, doing half time in the parlor and kitchen with the kids, half time on the porch with the old folks. They'd be nodding over the checkerboards, jumping each other's kings and yawning. Always talking about how we got to rise above this mess and don't tarry so long in the wilderness we forget how to fly. And don't let somebody start humming bout Zekial saw the wheel cause Granddaddy Sanderson would let loose.

"When we came to Africa, hear me now. I say when we came to Africa on the mother ship."

"Whatchu say?"

"Zekial saw it, he can tell you. He called it a wheel—well, that's his business."

And Miz Surrentine singing it out: "Way up in the middle of the aiiiirrr." Then dropping her chin back into the white lace collar she dresses every costume with. Eyes closed, the song vibrating in her chest, her bosom heaving and the words prying her mouth open again. "Zekial saw the wheel, way up in the middle of the air."

"I say when we came to Africa, we could fly. You heard me. We could fly." Granddaddy pointing a checker demanding to be crowned at Chester Hudson. "But we ate too much salt. Can't mess with too much salt cause it throws things out of proper balance. If you scientific, you know that. Ain't that right, Lacey?" tugging on my arm and I'm trying to empty the ashtrays but not too fast.

"And when the forces were all in balance, we were at the center of the field. The electro mag-net-tic field, I'm talking bout," rapping on the card table and waking up the dozers on the swing couch.

"Gravity? Don't be tellin me about no somesuch gravity. That ain't nuthin. We could fly. I'm tellin you something and I hope you listening. We could fly."

And Grandma Lyons stirring herself on the swing couch,

adjusting the pillows—beating them up, in fact. Clearing her throat to announce quite plainly, "But we ate salt. Ate too much salt."

Fess Newton, hearing his cue, launches into some fast-talking explanation of gravity, replete with positive and negative poles. Salt as a conductor. Too much as an inhibitor. Then Old Ma Hudson frowning up, her lips lost in the folds of cheek.

"If you can't dance it, Fess Newton. And if you can't sing it, Wade Sanderson, leastways tell it right. Tell it in terms of fire, water, air, earth and bone. It's the spirits that—"

"Same thing," Fess Newton hollering. "Forces is forces. We just using different names for—"

"Then tell it right with the right names for the things, stead of all this electro whatever. Make it sound like a coffeepot perkin. Can't nobody dance to that. My feet ain't even tapping. Was your foot tapping, Daddy?"

Grandpappy Lyons fast asleep. And he don't even stir when Bertha Washington leans over and slaps him across the knees with her trump tight hand.

"What wuz you saying, Sand," Bertha says, adjusting her buns on the skimpy chair, "fore Fess tried to steal your thunder?"

"I was saying that we could fly, but we got messed around with all that salt. Salt treks, salt trails, all those mother's tears, all those bones bleaching in the briny deep, all that sweat. Digging in the earth we became the salt of the earth. Couldn't pay us a salt, so they paid us a salary. Same thing. Too much salt—"

"Hold on," say Bertha, putting her hand down carefully. "You mean to tell me we shouldn't got paid? That's like saying we were well off as slaves."

"You miss my point, Sister Washington," Granddaddy Sanderson whisper, shaking his head all sorrowful-like. "All I'm

54

saying is we got grounded. Ain't been measuring our wingspan too much lately, as you'll notice. But we sure as hell got to rise above this here mess. We got to fly."

"Salt of the earth," somebody mumbles as I bring the tray of spiced tea in.

"The salt trails of a people," Sanderson resumes, "crisscrossing tracks down the road of history. And sometime they're scooped up like so much dust so we leave no trace. Scooped up to leave a lie in its place. And when you scoop a people's salt tracks up, you can lay em down somewhere else and misdirect the traffic. Or you can plunk down the whole bunch of salt and it be a stumblin block sure. Or you get it all sold back to you."

"You lost me there," Fess Newton say, using the opportunity to make a few devious moves on the board.

"Sure. They scoop em up, distill the stuff to crystals and sell ourselves back to us for seasoning so we can sweat some more. Seasoning. Did you hear me?"

"Ain't that just like white folks" comes the sigh from the swing couch.

"Hold it, hold it," demands Bertha. "Are you saying we eat our own history and that's a bad thing? Sound like a good thing to me."

"What he saying," Fess translates, "is that we eat our own footprints and that's too much salt."

"Footprints," Bertha snorts. "Sound like a foot's in the mouth somewhere in there. You got to talk plain, Sand. Your metaphors always so damn falutin. Talk plain, man."

"She tellin yawl something," Grandma Lyons say, sucking her lips together.

"I'm talking plain, sister. I'm tellin ya how it was and how it is. We get our sweat sold back to us so we can sweat some more. Sweat dripping in the white man's pails. Sweaty feet making tracks. Can I hep it if you igrant, Bertha?"

Bertha lays her hand down and cuts her eye at the old man, who grabs my arm, serious about communicating this idea. "You understand what I'm saying, Lacey. Maybe I got the words runnin too close together, but you know it's the truth. We salt eaters."

"I know why the Ethiopic is so salty, Lawd," Miz Surrentine starts calling.

"Hmmm, we know why the ocean be so salty," the response.

"But I sure as hell don't know why the Ethiopic is called the Atlantic." Fess Newton mashes in a line that just won't scan. But don't nobody pay him no mind. They continue singing the song.

"They sleep in the deep, sated with salt."

"How many you suspect? How many?" the call.

"Many thousands gone," the reply. "Many thousands gone."

Jason is shaking my arm loose of his so he can step in front of me for a full face look.

"Are you going off, Lacey?"

"Just thinking, Jason. I need another sixties. The energy of the seventies just don't do me nuthin. Was I growling again?"

"Humming. I think you need a vacation. You haven't taken a vacation in years," he mumbles, looking over the park all snowy white.

The park is usually a shortcut to the Lenox Lake Apartments. But no one's made a path through yet. Vincent and his baby brother Roger venture into the drift and are up to their knees in no time.

"We got to go the long way round," says Abdul, yanking Roger back by his hood. "Come on now, fore you get lost in there."

"We going by the Jiffy Mart, Ndugu Jason?"

Jason nods and Malaika jumps up and down, the top crust of snow splintering every which way in sparkles all the way to my feet.

"Yeeeey, hot chocolate, hot chocolate." The kids jack-rabbit down the sidewalk, leaving us a scattered path to follow.

There're about two or three slits of glass visible of the Jiffy Mart's window. Taped centerfolds of the weekly community paper announce a sale on Beech-Nut baby foods and ground chuck and some brand of mouthwash I never heard of. Handmade signs on shiny white butcher paper says now is the time to stock up on GE bulbs and Hudson paper towels. Cling peaches are going for forty-eight cents a can. Oxtails are so high I quit reading.

The kids are doing a drill-team number on the tiles that mark the border between the Jiffy Mart fountain and the Jiffy Mart grocery section. Abdul is snuffling and snorting snot, executing the most intricate katas while Baby Roger slaps out the beat on the vinyl stools. Me and Jason press up against two slits of glass and make funny faces. But when you're inside and warm and the hot chocolate is already whizzing in the mixer, you just ain't thinking to look outside at your teachers gone bananas. The wind pushes at our backs and shoves us through the door into a solid, sudden wall of heat.

"I'd better call Malaika's daddy," I say, "and find out what time he's picking her up from work. Whose house shall I—?"

"Look," Vincent hollers over to me, "real cups!" He taps the cups, trying to make them ring. He knows I am a sucker for a real cup.

"I guess they had to recall all the polystyrene cups, Vincent."

"For napalm, I bet," he mutters, the smile gone. "To kill the Vietnamese children."

The kids crowd around Vincent, who is eight and the oldest

kid at the school. He gives a mini-lecture on the war while me and Jason ease up to the counter across the sloppy tile. The fountain is empty except for us. The waitress stops staring at the clock to say hello. The grocery is jam-packed.

"Ain't that the widder man and his son, Lacey?" Jason asks.

Gregory the Younger's at the check-out counter, 15¢ tomato paste in hand, minor fortune of crops stuffed in his duffel coat if I know Greg. Gregory the Elder's in the meat department cattle-rustling, paying the butcher man no mind. Some irate lady's all up in the butcher's face, jabbing at the cellophaned steaks, demanding he swear on his dead mother's soul that there's more meat than gristle and bone under the red dye.

"You want me to cut you a steak?" the butcher groans, swinging the door open to the back and ushering her in. "Why you got to put me through all these changes every time you come in here, Mrs. Harper. All you got to do is ring the bell. I told you once, I told you a thousand times . . ."

Gregory the Elder is steady shoving steaks down his outsized pants.

"Bold son of a bitch, ain't he?" Jason's leaning back on the counter, waiting for his chocolate to cool. "I saw him get caught once in the hardware store. Don't you know he convinced the people they were doing some racist hallucinating."

"He's got talent, Jason. Talent."

·"Uhh-huhn." Jason's blowing into his cup, undecided whether to admire or be appalled. Or maybe he's trying to figure out how to put this talent in the service of the people. And I can see the sign posted outside the school: *The Harriet Tubman Institute of Struggle Presents the Thieves of Watts Circle in a Lecture-Demonstration, Part 3 in the Series of Survival Technique Seminars. Donations Requested But Not Mandatory; Hell, These Is Hard Times. Special Workshop to Follow on How to Rip Off General Motors, U.S. Steel and Other Superthief Corporations.*

"This got calcium in it for teeth and bones, and vitamins and protein for growth," Vincent is instructing, "on account of the milk."

"We already know that," Abdul says.

"It got brown stuff too," says Roger. "What it good for?"

"Is the chocolate good for us or bad, Ndugu Jason?" Malaika asks.

"It's cool," Jason mumbles, preoccupied with the Gregorys.

"Mine's hot," she says, eyeing her teacher suspiciously.

Gregory the Elder's pants cuff is coming up out of his left boot. There's a pool of blood forming around his feet. His pants leg stained and people noticing. The old man glances down and cool as you please limps forward and taps the woman at the head of the line, grimacing to beat the band.

"Scuse me," he moans. "Can I go through?" He holds up a lone can of beer and winces. "I gotta get home and change these bandages. I think the doctor discharged me way too soon."

The woman's hand is poised over the piled-high basket. She looks at the leg, the stain, then toward the folks clustered around the pool of blood mumbling, then steps aside for the old gent and nods to the cashier. Jason bangs his cup down and spins around full face. The mirror behind the malt machine just ain't picking up enough of the scene to suit him. Gregory the Elder pays for his beer and stiff-leg limps out the Jiffy Mart, his son rushing forward and bending just in time to catch a leaky steak dropping down the chute of them fat-man pants.

"Work your show," I sigh. But Jason's still undecided about it all. I'm waiting for him to throw the question open for the kids to discuss. And I'm eager to hear how they'll unravel the ethics of stealing these days. Months before, I had read them an excerpt from "Scoring" in Huey Newton's book, and we had a pretty lively discussion. But I can't recall just what positions they took on the matter.

Jason opens his mouth and I give full attention, expecting him to begin orchestrating the discussion. But instead he turns to me and asks kind of dreamily, "Seen the Rafer boys lately?"

"Heard they got caught flat out trying to take off a whole house on Bedford Valley Drive."

"Big Rafer subject to take his mama off," says Jason.

Jason had barred the Rafer boys from the school and from the radio station where the kids do weekly programing. Big Rafer's just not discriminating at all. The three middle boys tend to steal when they're pressed for cash. The twins steal strictly from white folks, which would be cool, I guess, except they do it for all the wrong reasons, cause they truly believe white folks are better—are better and got to pay for that fact. I make a note to think this through and revive the scoring discussion.

"We got twelve minutes to get Abdul to the radio station," Vincent says, gazing up at the clock over the banana split dishes. The waitress glances up, slips her foot in and out of her shoe, glances at her watch, then out at the snow, groans.

"You the kid that gives the weather reports?" she asks Abdul.

Abdul nods and she smiles. "You give a good weather report," she says. "Wish I had listened to you yesterday." She stares out of the window, ducking, feinting, tipping, trying to see through the cracks and slits of clear glass.

"Whatchu gonna say tonight?" she asks, leaning her elbows on the counter.

Abdul rummages around in his pockets and pulls out an

index card. He lip-reads a while, then shoves it back in his jacket. "Well, mostly I'll tell people to get their mittens out, to wear a cap with ear flaps, and to scoop up two fingers of Vaseline, cause tomorrow gonna be meaner than today."

"Oh, Lord," she sighs, pushing away from the counter and checking the clock again. "And the night-shift girl ain't even here."

"See ya," the kids wave and she waves and we nod and scoot out into the cold.

The wind at least is at our backs when we come out of the funeral home that houses the community radio station. The kids wave up at Abdul and his aunt in the window, coats off, looking warm, one block from home and a car too. Pop Sellars pulls up in his Caddy and waves too, ducking in the building and not offering us a lift.

"Well, at least he's not still trying to press lollipops on the kids," Jason jokes, reading my mind. "Or trying to corner you back there with the mummies talking about his sherry collection and cordial glasses from Florence, Italy."

"Florence, France, Jason. He always says Florence, France."

The wind's not the problem, but the dark is. Look like half the streetlights are out and it's damn spooky. And no matter how hard I try to shorten the distance between the Sellars' and the Taylor boys' home, it just won't shorten.

"I can't keep up, Admiral," I shout breathlessly. "Just park me here by this tree and send a dog sled back for my body. The expedition must go on."

I lean against a mailbox, staring at the one streetlamp halo. I feel like I can really lean thus for years.

"Just a few more steps, Dada Lacey," Vincent coaxes. "And we can plant the flag at the pole."

"Which flag?" Malaika asks, ready to correct.

"The liberation flag. Hah!" And they trot off, Baby Roger running six steps for each of their one.

"I've got one bullet left, Admiral . . . in case . . . the wolves . . ."

"Will you cut it out, Lacey. It's starting to blizzard." Jason is behind me now, shoving me ahead. I can't tell if I'm kidding or not. My legs are not there. Something inside is loose and knocking around.

"Brandy. Brandy . . . I need some brandy. Where's the damn Saint Bernard? Never there when you need him. Probably pissing on some Alpine skier dead in the drift." I could use more than brandy.

"Buck up, kid. Just around the bend's a relief station if you're serious about that brandy," Jason says so soberly I'm scared of myself.

But just around the bend's the bedlam station, Darnell's Bar and Grill, where folks go in to go right off. Two dudes are duking in shirt sleeves cold as it is, wrassling each other all over the sidewalk, and the kids are scooting by one by one. Folks are peeping through the freeze patterns of Darnell's big window, toasting these fools banging each other all up into the mailbox, slamming each other into Darnell's door, which shows you what can happen to tropical folk in the snow, cause Darnell subject to ram a fist in your eye for just talking bad about his joint, much less coming close to loosening hinges.

"Why they got to off on each other? They need to go over to that African art exhibit and do the guards in. You know I do believe them guards had orders to shoot anybody that touched the masks and stuff. Did you see how he shouted me down when I fussed at him for yelling at the kids? Where the hell were you, Jason, come to think of it?"

"Is that what sent you off, Lacey? Some white boy got the

power to short-circuit your system? Damn. You do need a vacation."

"Aww shit, Jason. It's everything." I look back over my shoulder at the whole block and damn if the two gladiators ain't ripped the clothes off each other's backs and are now gnashing their teeth and falling all over people's cars. The one in the Italian neorealism undershirt got the other flung back over the hood of a police car.

"Madness."

"What'll get you straight again, Lacey? You need a drink?"

"I need to kill me somebody, I think."

"Too late. You've been committed to development, not murder. Should have thought of that earlier before you made your choice of career."

"Well, the guidance counselor never mentioned—"

"You some crazy woman, Lacey. Next you'll be arguing that I'm advocating a reactionary division of labor, right?"

"Right. I can be in the teacher corps and on the assassin squad too."

Jason throws back his head and howls. Been knowing him off and on for ten years and can count the times he's laughed like that. He mostly gives you a dry attic rustly sound or a deep basement grunt. I guess that's why we've been friends rather than lovers. I can love a man who thinks and lives and works like Jason. But for shonuff loving the man got to know how to laugh his ass off. Jason is still laughing, and he's gradually getting attractive in a whole new way. I'm trying to hold my frozen jaws steady. My chattering teeth bout to shake me loose from my frame. Then we turn the corner into the wind and there's no more talking. So I got to put on hold what I want to say to him about how laughing becomes him, how laughing suits me. It's too cold to think warmly. Which gives me insight into the European. Where else would colonialism, slavery, capitalism come from except out of the icebox.

"You got provisions at your place, Father?"

Jason nods, but it's clear he's not following me. He assumes I am asking for Malaika's sake, though neither one of us can figure out whose turn it is to take the kid till her daddy gets off work. But if we can't figure it out, then maybe daddy can't either and will call both places. So really don't matter.

The entrance to Lenox Lake Apartments is for drivers, not walkers. We skid over the brake bumpers hidden in the snow and got to keep shouting to the kids to move over cause the cars whiz around there in that narrow road, bumpers or no.

"Come on, slowpokes," the kids are calling, taking a shortcut through some bushes on the perimeter of the lake. Me and Jason find ourselves slowing down, looking past the basketball court to the new high school beyond a cyclone fence. It right away reminds me, and Jason too I figure, of the Job Corps centers we had to rescue our tutors from five years back. This school looks exactly like the prison it was meant to be.

Without warning the children come racing into us and I fail to brace myself and wind up on my ass. I take it for a sign.

"Sorry," Vincent says, and they all huddle to get me off the ground. "My sister can't stand that school," he spits with passion. "Makes her feel real bad to be in there, she says."

"That's the whole point," I say, dusting powder from my coat.

The five of us stand there in the sparkling dark staring at the school behind the fence. Cement grounds, hard, cold, treeless, shadowless, no hiding places or clustering places for plotting and scheming or just getting together. The building squat on an angle, as though snubbing the rest of the neighborhood, giving a cold shoulder, isolating itself, separating its inmates from the rest of the folks. And no windows. We crunch silently to the apartment building, hushed.

"I'd like to get my hands on . . . " I'm growling again in the suffocating lobby where hot air laced with coffee makes its assault on my system.

"What would you do, Dada Lacey, when you got your hands on those people?"

I grab Baby Roger's scarf and twist and snarl and bite and spit. They all do me one better, strangling themselves and flinging their bodies all over the hall, till it finally occurs to Vincent that he's too old for this. He sobers up and presses the elevator button and gives me a look. I straighten up.

Jason laughs as we tumble into the elevator gagging, choking, gasping. I catch myself examining the cage for telltale perforations. The gas valve'd be behind the center panel. And at the precise moment, the elevator will stop between floors, and one press on the emergency button will trigger the release of the lethal gas.

"Lacey, we need a lesson on architectural design. The politics of arch—"

"Got it."

"Is your car still in the shop, Dada Lacey? That why we had to walk?"

"Walking's good for you," Vincent tells his brother. "A lot of things you can't see in the community if you riding."

"What wrong with your car?" Baby Roger asks.

"Transmission," I mumble and leave it to Jason and Vincent to translate. Needs to be fitted out with a diesel engine, I do not say. Extra gas reserves, bulletproof glass, aquatic wings. Hard times and getting harder every day, and soon the state won't be able to deliver up race, class, caste, skin privileges. And what ya offer when ya got no more dazzling trinkets or fish sandwiches? Niggers, that's what. Hard times and getting harder every and still the people will not see. See but don't trust their eyes. Trust but won't take responsibility for their eyes. And when will conditions be riper to strike?

"Lacey."

Children waiting to grow up, spread out, leap forward, soar. When? All the babies on the way. When? Ancestors bleaching in the deep. When? Conditions been ripe. When?

"Dada Lacey?"

When? Before amnesia sets in and all families turn to cargo cults. All taboos and all restraints gone. Children bludgeoning their mamas. Anything goes. When? Half the world to be freed up. When?

"What kind of car is it?"

"I'm absent," I remember to say to Vincent, who requests clarity of that kind.

"It's orange," Vincent answers for me.

"When you ride in an orange car, Baby Roger," Malaika instructs, "you ride around in circles."

"That's a pun," Jason says, holding the door open. "You asked me to point one out, Vincent. Remember?"

Vincent purses his lips. He doesn't remember, but he's certain it will connect. He is a patient little brother, patient and thorough. He nods and holds the door for Jason.

Sister Jennifer's holding the apartment door open with her behind, steady shoveling forkfuls of cabbage into the shadow beneath her denim cap yanked low. The fork clanking on the saucer echoes loud in the hallway.

"Mama says to tell ya the pot's on," she says to us, sucking in to let her brothers past. "You want coffee, dinner?"

What I want is an iron lung and two weeks in the tropics. Can't survive another two days of the ice age. I feel marsh gas swamping through me. Brimming over, I'll be dangerous to ignite.

"Naaw, but thanks," Jason is trying to say, backing out the way of the kids romping back and forth doing last tag. "We gotta get goin." He tries to grab Malaika to interrupt the routine guaranteed to spin into a thirty-minute number unchecked.

"Last tag," Vincent roars, scurrying into the apartment for the third time, his sister plastered against the door holding the plate high up over traffic danger.

All the way down I'm miserable about Jennifer. The Institute has yet to provide a point of entry for the teens, and that's a serious error, a waste all around. They'd make such good teachers. Each one teach one, as Dada Swan says, develop through sharing, develop through developing others. I stumble off the elevator feeling underdeveloped. Frozen, scattered, cynical, I'm slipping back into the slime.

"What'll we do with that ugly school after?" Malaika's saying, blocking our way out with her arms so we have to "play," though it's not a game, Lord knows it ain't no game, but part of the training to keep the vision vibrant under all the deadening weight heaped high on it every day and every day and every.

"It could be a wing of the Museum of the Revolution," Jason says.

Malaika's arms are wings now, she glides around us, certain we'll stay put till she comes full circle. Jason is gazing past the fence and actually seeing it in sunlight. The people in line, chatting, jovial, eager to see how it was, what conditions used to be like, what they use to not all the times see though was there.

"We can put the Crimes Against the People Section in it.

67

The building's perfect for it, don't you think, Lacey?"

Promise? I want to ask. Except I want it to mean too much. Like promise, yeah, but promise too to be ready to call it a dream tomorrow if we've miscalculated altogether. Promise all kind of ways and angles so I can trudge on through this crystalline wonder tonight, the ugly slush tomorrow. You can depend on Jason, can bank on what he has to do, say, see. Nobody ever asks a Jason what it ain't in them to deliver. Deliver, us, Jason. That's stupid. Pitiful. I feel salt on my lips.

"My nana says making old people have to eat dog food and be alone and scared on account of all them stairs and no light bulbs in the hall, she say that's a crime."

"All of that'll be in the museum," Jason says through his teeth.

Malaika gets between us and we trot past the lake, a marshy mess man built to give the apartments a name and the rents a boost. I'm holding myself round with the free arm as though to catch up whatever it is I've let slip and is dragging me from my juicy face down.

"And will all the children go to schools like ours?"

"Yes," we say, smiling down into her upturned face.

"I can help teach the little *little* kids," she says, pulling us closer. "Cause I can read now and I know my numbers and my colors and my notes. And I can share. I know how to share."

We hug her, each other through her. I hug myself. I'm sagging. If I choose to say something else I won't be heard. They won't hear me. I'm in solitary confinement. Limbo. Not there where they are. And not where I used to be, have moved forever from that place. Would just be hollering into the toilet bowl for the echo of my own voice.

It is snowing straight down now, the wind dying. We hear our crunching across the sparkling crust amplified, precise. So very much in the present. Centered.

"Will the new time come soon, Ndugu Jason? Will the people free the country soon?" Her tongue is out catching snowflakes. She's nonchalant about listening. Her training answers what there is to answer. Cross-eyed she checks the landing of each flake as though on the lookout for one particular, a sign.

"It's here already," Jason says, staring at her. "Because the new people, the new commitment, the new way is already here."

"In our lifetime?" she persists.

"In our lifetime."

Promise? I want to demand, like the whole weight is his. She scoots out from between us, whirling, eating. Me and Jason lock arms and he's steering me in the direction of his place.

"We won't mind the snow and the wind then," she sings. "Cause everybody'll have warm clothes and we'll all trust each other and can stop at anybody's house for hot chocolate cause won't nobody be scared or selfish. Won't even be locks on the doors. And every sister will be my mother. Right, Dada Lacey?"

"Yeah," I say, but it don't buoy me up. I'm drooping, sagging.

The two of them are looking up as the moon comes out, Jason unhooking his arm to whirl around on his heel like he's executing a new figure. I'm in a free fall now, dropping through layers and layers of the spangled dark. I feel the ground coming up, the snow bursting into stars at my feet too close.

"I promise," I mutter, waiting for a surge of energy to lift. "I promise."

It's their arms I feel finally straightening me up on both sides. Their arms and their selves.

"Let's hurry," they whisper, dragging me along in the night.

THE
SEA
BIRDS
ARE
STILL
ALIVE

Newspapers swirled around the deck. Sheets of print sucked up under the boat's tin roofing, shredded, then dropped into the water. A centerfold—ragged from its windswept journey across feet, between the bench legs, in and out among the closely woven baskets—smacked up flat against the side railings, buzzing loudly. Eyes swiveled away from the cabin of the pilot, whose whistle had just warned a freighter turning too widely. But the ensnared paper vibrating against the rusty rails held attention for only a moment. Some on board could read the script. Others couldn't read at all. For most, it didn't matter what the censored papers chose to say. The situation was confused enough without reports from the government press.

Rebel forces in the countryside have been subdued, it would say in the morning. By evening the wiped-out forces were reported in control of two villages. A particularly menacing commando unit were now prisoners of the Americans, one paper would say. Another would claim that victory for the Royal Army. Turmoil in the city was attributed to roving bandits on page one, to foreign paid provocateurs on page two, then denied altogether on page three. Everything under control, the papers boasted.

But someone, perhaps students stirred up by the Chinese professors at the universities, had made attacks on the embassies, said the papers. And someone in national uniform—unemployed actors, perhaps—had been raiding the markets extorting fees and molesting women. Everything under control. As for the disruption of the prince's birthday celebration, clearly that was the work of juvenile delinquents, and parents needed to exert more control. A recent issue of the daily laid the city disturbances at the feet of irresponsible women whose husbands would be fined.

The country woman in a long, striped skirt kicked at the papers caught between her baskets and spat betel juice in the prince's face. He flew over the side, disgraced. Some passengers laughed, others scowled. The old grandmother on her haunches plucked at the long, striped skirt for attention, then shared her toothless grin with any one else who cared to join them in their daring ridicule of royalty.

Eyes speckled and rimmed red, the grandmother studied the old gentleman on the side bench before her. He would neither smile nor scowl. He simply sat, his soft cloth shoes spread open in a V, a long clay pipe cold in his hand. The old woman looked again and saw that his other hand was missing. In a schoolteacher gesture that flooded where her memory of schooldays should have been, he ran a hand lazily over his jaw, worrying the hairs sprouting from his chin. She scanned his soft cloth suit for patriotic pins, wondering which war had martyred him, had pulled him from his classroom and left some district untutored. He sat straight and proud, one hand, chin whiskers, cold pipe. Her smile was different now. He had come to the end of his tobacco, but he had, she thought, much face left.

The vendors, mostly young children and the very old, checked the straps on their wooden trays, fussed over the paper cones of nuts and beans, the hanks of shoelaces, the tins of balms and nostrums, the rice-paper blobs of caramels. They sat cross-legged on the deck together, backs against the pilot's cabin. They chatted, ignoring the newspapers swirling around their wares.

The refugees kept watch over their belongings, slapping at the newspapers tangled round their feet, bunching up between the bundles of their household goods. Whatever explanation the papers offered, the situation meant for them upheaval and poor payment for the things too big to transport.

The country woman in the long, striped skirt squatted among her baskets and gave the sour curds a shake. She unwrapped her waistband, planning out her errands of the day, and wound the cloth around the old grandmother's head brushed bald by the wind lunging through the rails. Looking around at the foreigners, lip curling, the country woman spat in the direction of two new black shoes.

The foreigners glanced at the spit, at the soldier near the pilot's cabin who would not look, at the pairs and pairs of dark eyes, and sat. Newspapers tumbled unnoticed over their briefcases and shoes. Their situation was never recounted in those papers. Racing from country to country, exchanging currency from one that looked like stage money to another just as unreal, convinced they were being cheated, certain they were being mistreated, body alert for pickpockets, feet stinging from leather shoes, back stiff to insult or argument that their respective governments had committed unspeakable crimes, vile and filthy deeds.

Queuing up on endless lines for visas, permits, letters of transit. Trying to read an overseas newspaper for some trace of their own situation and finding none there either. The only attention, sardonic and scathing, in the rebel press, of all places. Slumped over for hours on hard benches at airports or railroad terminals or in offices where people spat and soldiers looked in the other direction. This soldier with blanked eyes and face staring off toward the horizon, a flurry of newspaper encircling his head. The foreigners sat, windblown, despised.

The pilot bent to stuff newspapers in his shoes to muffle the vibrations from the engine. For him the situation meant doubled-up hours transporting trucks and baggage and soldiers and an endless array of passengers ever anxious about the possibility of mines in the waters. The papers assured daily in increasingly strident tones that there was nothing to fear. But daily the people gathered on the jetties to watch the divers surface with one more mine the Americans were supposed to have removed.

The screech of sea birds made all heads turn toward the back of the boat. There a young girl, reckless near the edge where the wind swept in to balloon her clothes out and threatened to lift her from the deck, was flinging food to the birds who swooped and squabbled in scattered formation, flapping greedily after the rusting boat, snatching morsels out of the air one hair away from the foam churned high by the boat paddles. Or suspended in midair awaited the next pitch of bread, trying to fend off, without losing prime position in front of the girl, the rest of the flock, picking, clutching, nicking a wing, an eye.

One bird now in a downward spiral, beak overloaded, neck broken, wailing, then disappearing from view in a flurry of claws.

The passengers near the back of the boat where the tin roof ended and the full force of the wind began mumbled disapproval. Poor people starving in the countryside, starving in the cities, oxen too weak to pull a plow, chickens too scrawny to bother, and here right before their eyes good food wasted on worthless birds.

Two hill women on their straw mats, needles poised over the patches they snipped and stitched hurriedly, looked up, then sank their heads in sorrow over the waste of food. Quickly they picked up their pace. If they didn't hurry, they'd have nothing to sell. Nothing to sell, then nothing to eat and nothing to wear. They'd be run in their rags from the hotels where foreigners jingled loose change. Canadians, Americans, Australians, Europeans picking over their work and sneering, stalking away in dazzling shoes or staying to haggle ruthlessly in broken tongues. One of the women stabbed herself cruelly to fix her mind on the work at hand. To substitute for the pain she felt hopeless to deal with, with a pain she could understand.

A young man with a hard, brown face leaned over the rail to spit. Not at the girl and the wanton waste, but in answer to the Frenchwoman's question was he making his home in the city. Home. In '46 when the United States notified the families their island was needed for nuclear tests, he'd been a child peeping through the chinks in the bamboo awning, peeping at shells along the seashore. He couldn't even walk yet, much less protest. And the islanders, bowed down by centuries of servitude to the Spanish, the French, the Japanese, the Americans, complied.

The lovely atoll that was home devastated by two decades of atomic, then hydrogen, blasts. For years, with no compensation money, they waited for an unseen needle on an unknown gauge to record the radiation level and announce it safe to return home. They waited, complied, were rerouted, resettled at this camp or that island, the old songs gone, the dances forgotten, the elders and the ancient wisdoms put aside, the memory of home scattered in the wind.

Home for him had been a memory of yellow melons and the elders with their tea sitting right outside his window under the awning. Home after that, a wicker basket and his father's uncle's pallet in muddy tent cities, flooded wooden barracks, compounds with loudspeakers but no vegetation and no work to keep one's dignity upright. Meager rations in one country, hostility in the next.

Then finding home among islanders who remembered home, a color, a sound, the shells, the leaping fish, the cool grottoes. And home among other people foreign but not foreign, people certain that humanity was their kin, the world their home. Home with people like that who shared their next-to-nothing things and their more-than-hoped-for wealth of spirit. Home with people who watched other needles on other gauges that recorded the rising winds.

The young man with the hard, brown face leaned over the rail, the wind shoving his hair flat like that earlier wind had bowed the island grasses down outside his window. But one sturdy stem had remained upright; dark green, defiant, it had imprinted indelibly on his brain. The young man smiled, the wind drawing his lips back, baring his teeth. It was a good time in history to be on the earth, to be on the boat going home. He leaned way over, examining the holes below that bled rust with each grumble of the engine, each turn of the wooden paddles. Then he straightened, back stiff with the conviction that he, like many others going home now, was totally unavailable for servitude.

The notebook pages fluttered and threatened to fly off in the wind. The correspondent leafed through, the heels of her hands holding down the months and months of notes. Her mouth full of paper clips, she tried to make some order and find a section of blank papers that would get her through the stage she now anticipated: agricultural, commercial, industrial operations, foreign and domestic, taken over by a provisional revolutionary authority. She flipped through the filled pages.

. . . summit conferences . . . cloak and dagger . . . solidarity banners . . . May I see your papers? . . . ginger candy with too many hairs for eating . . . crepe-paper flowers for the dead . . . sabotage at the plants . . . mass arrests . . .

. . . Your papers, please . . . ox collars turned plant hangers priced for tourists and not farmers . . . Sorry, no journalists allowed . . . borders closed . . . defections in the army . . . the people's militia growing every day . . . the Indian widow in endless exile having disgraced her family rejecting suttee, knocking on her hotel door with another nightmare to relate, haunted by her husband still burning on the funeral pyre . . . bellboys peeking through the transom . . . hauled before the secret police and questioned about the other foreigners in the hotels . . . double agents . . .

. . . the Slavic woman at the Exchange in harlequin glasses from Hollywood and plastic wedgies from the Caribbean . . . babies wrapped in newspapers dying near their dying mothers on floors of prison cells . . . braziers in the street and families huddled round roasting rat, some people said . . . the Ugandan diplomat in alligator shoes holdin forth in the café bar . . . the landlord's daughter caught in a roundup, for the rally had been held right outside her dressmaker's shop, heard the revolution was coming and the rich would be slaughtered, blackened her teeth and sold the family treasures in the market, parceled out the lands to the tenants and waited for the revolution to come, bitter that none came in two weeks she returned to the estate looking for a dentist and a handout . . .

. . . Your letters of introduction, please . . . parachutes overhead and the people fleeing, expecting bombs, missiles of some sort or another, the packages floating down could perhaps be medicines or leaflets; coming out of hiding they discover boxes of brandied peaches and tinned pheasant marked for the general in the district . . . Your identification card, please . . .

. . . USAID officers in the company of known assassins . . . death squadrons . . . torture quotas . . . students rounded up on the steps of the university library . . . sentences but not trial notes posted under glass outside municipal buildings . . . schoolboys and merchants on the army payroll . . . the arrest of the schoolteacher who'd led her to the DMZ then mysteriously turned waxworks . . .

She had logged incessantly, sent numerous cables to the wire service, conducted interviews in caves, in hallways, in swamps in the dead of night under fire, translated graffiti on the walls of paramilitary organizations under the guise of manufacturing plants seized by the student-worker coalition, decoded purloined documents her paper grumbled about paying for, ignored the summons home. She could not go home now, not yet, not when the victory of the people was so close at hand.

She closed the looseleaf and zippered it tight. She had missed Paris in the spring of '68. She would not miss this moment of history emerging right before her eyes. Cadres pouring into the cities from the liberated zones, organizing women, students, workers boldly in view of the demoralized national troops. She could write now as she never had before. Her earlier work so like the travel posters over her desk in Paris, interesting but didn't mean she'd been there.

She was there now. She felt she was already in the mobilized city. Could feel herself shoving through the revolving doors of the Imperial Palace Hotel, which some joked should be called the Anti-Imperialist Hotel. Heels clicking over the tile, tongue clumsy with the language, cautious with the questions, certain in the times. A room with no transom. The view of the streets and the cadres at outdoor rallies. "Why are our people poor?" they would begin. She felt she was already there, in the moment.

The little girl feeding the birds bumped the correspondent out of her reverie and excused herself in French, much to the woman's surprise. But of course. The correspondent examined the clothes, the black hair, the round face with the dark eyes and high cheekbones, and remembered where she was. She clutched the precious cargo in her lap, spitting out one twisted paper clip that skidded over the deck, then disappeared over the side. She ignored the wind, the squawling birds, the little girl. She was also unaware of the soldier who now watched her in convoluted hatred.

On the long bench by the pilot's cabin, the American sat amid a muddle of luggage, his own and the bags of poor folk crowding him. Eight years, he was thinking, eight damn years making a name for myself in the Department of the Interior, learning the languages almost of the Midwest Indians, and now transferred to some godforsaken outpost in the middle of east hell. An encampment where he'd oversee the refugees evacuated by the United States in its war against the Reds. He'd been told at orientation that the last typhoon of salt water had caved in the dikes and swept away the agricultural project, so he'd have to start from scratch. What did he know about constructing dikes or irrigating land and suchlike?

They'd run him through a crash course of languages and cultures, but hadn't explained much about the agricultural project, except that he was to see to it that the dike was built and the cyclone fence repaired at once. He ran a hand across his bristly face and smiled. It had been quite a course. But then he frowned, thinking of all the papers he'd had to sign, declarations of discretion, secrecy. No one at the Defense Department had answered to his satisfaction the charges about germ and chemical research being conducted at the camp. It wasn't just the troublemakers this time making those charges. Rumors were rife even in responsible Washington circles.

He looked around the boat. The people, the rusting hulk, the birds caterwauling in the rear. When he'd missed his plane and lost contact with the other new officers headed for the camp, he'd waited foolishly in the airport for word from them. But scientists were like that—brisk, brusque, cold. And so he'd had to make his own way to the post. And why so many scientists? Twenty years before when he'd joined the service, Red China and North Korea had accused the United States of germ warfare. He'd known that for a lie. Germ warfare was a violation of international law, after all. But this time . . . and responsible people . . . and those biochemists were scheduled to work only three-hour shifts in the infirmary . . . He hugged his briefcase.

His briefcase bulged with material he was to release in flyers, bark out over loudspeakers, feed to the press. Toxic fallout from defoliants does not endanger the health, the flyers argued. As for the charges of germ warfare, so much enemy propaganda, the material said. But do not eat shellfish, other flyers said, and avoid deep-root vegetables. And check in at the dispensary once a month, it warned in bold caps.

The American rearranged his body on the hard bench and wondered who was sitting in his leather chair back in Washington. He yearned to kick off his shoes, buzz for a drink, bury his stocking feet in the deep, gray carpet. Exasperated, chilled, unshaven, knees aching, he stretched, cocky in the knowledge that Pine Ridge Reservation would never have been disrupted had he been at his desk. They'd see. He'd be recalled. Twenty-eight years of good service. Eight years at the Interior and now outside, put out to pasture. He'd be recalled. They'd see.

His eyes rested for a moment on the blob of brown spit near his shoes and then he studied the passengers again, testing himself. He'd been tutored with stacks of *National Geographic* to enable him to distinguish the various stocks of people indigenous to the Mekong, the Indian Ocean, the Pacific. Hue, eye size and slant, bone structure, hairline. But looking round the deck, he was forced to frown again. For other than the French-woman and other obvious Europeans, everyone looked like the Indians from Minnesota or the Hawaiians on TV or the Mexicans recently moved into his daughter's neighborhood. The children's eyes didn't even have a hint of slant. He thought of the two colored children who'd gone to his son's high school. Did their eyes suddenly slant after graduation?

The pilot pulled his cap down to watch undetected the fat man by the coil of ropes, leaning into the wind looking like an ancient Victory from the schoolbooks or the statue winging the grill of the Mercedes below deck. It was the landlord from his district, impatient to get back to civilization. The landlord who made the crossing once a year at election time, who would arrive in the district in traditional dress, the incongruous leather shoes mocking the ploy. The press at his elbow, his assistants assembling the people, he would promise an irrigation pump and the new road once more. The press out of earshot, he would threaten to evict the farmers from the land.

Prodded by the landlord's assistants, the people would line up to shake the fat hand, to deposit their votes on yellow slips of paper into his beefy paw. Then stepping back, he would turn and march with his entourage back to the jetty. He was now returning to the city in the Western suit worn under the costume, his Mercedes below deck with the tithes of rice and chickens he always collected, the sticky black boxes the tribesmen brought down from the hills, the sacks of grain for brew the landlord himself had outlawed in the district.

The pilot clenched his jaws and gripped the wheel rather than crash through the cabin window and throttle the fat man. No impulsive actions, the cadres had cautioned the people. Timing and patience, collective push, discipline. It would be a long war, had been a long war. The pilot could not remember a time of peace except in the words of the old songs. But soon the people would confront the rich grown fat off the blood and bones of the people. Would accuse them face to face in the people's tribunals. It was just a matter of time and the reign of terror would be over and life could start anew. The landlords, the war lords, the imperialists were no match for the force of the people, the force of justice, once the people moved together.

The pilot yanked his cap lower and straightened over the wheel. He could be patient. The leaders spoke wisdom to the people and shared their hardships. And he would do his part, no longer envious of their leadership. He watched the churning waters, proud of his part in history. For as the master pilot often said to him, it's not the water in front that pulls the river along. It's the rear guard that is the driving force.

The pilot thought of the rear guard. Thought of the widow woman who hid the cadres in her storage sheds and under her hut, who cooked for the young men of the district, proud in her hatred for the enemy, proud in her love for the country and the nation coming soon. She was doing her part filling up the quivers with new arrows, rosining the twine for the crossbow, stirring in the pot where the poison brewed.

And no one told her any more that that was no way to defend the district, not against B-52's and F 1104's, incendiary gels and M-16's. No one told her that any more, not after she had ambushed the soldiers who'd penetrated their line. No one told her, for the widow woman had and would again, had been taught she could and should by the fighters before her cutting arrows in the crawl space under the huts of old, sharpening arrowheads by the light of trapped-firefly lanterns, chanting the war songs and the old prayers and the new creeds of allegiance to a new day, urging the children to hurry with the branches, the branches and the mud hens, for an offering had to be burned on the temple steps. No one told the widow woman not to, even now when the temple steps were green-black with soil mold, slick with greasy votives. For the widow woman was the vessel of the old stratagems, a walking manual, having lost a grandfather, a father, six uncles, four sons, two husbands, and a daughter to the French, the Japanese, the Americans. No one told her not to, for the district was too busy listening as she related, stirring in the pots, how the people of old planted stakes in the waters to ensnare and wreck the enemy ships.

The pilot looked away from the water and back to the landlord. Watched him hard till his image faded and the vision of the women of old feeding arrows into the men's quivers blurred with the image of the young girls of his district feeding bullet belts into the guns.

What sounded like the twang of a bowstring made the pilot

twist round toward the back of the boat. Strained heads lifted passengers from the benches, eager to see for themselves what the frenzied woman and the little girl were doing. With wire from her unbound hair, the mother of the girl whipped in slashing motions, slicing rust from the rails, ripping feathers from the birds, making siren sounds with the wire that recalled for most aboard the long nights of shelling. Two students leaned their packs against the side railings and rushed forward stamping, flapping their jackets, bellowing the birds away. In a scatter the birds flew off.

Birds will get vicious when they're fed and then rejected, thought the researcher, fishing out a pen to take notes. People as well, he mused, then nodded agreement with the notion. The chaotic situation in the country was just that: natives supported by foreign aid, sustained, educated, taught a superior way of life, strike out in adolescent pique when abandoned. "The Dependency Complex of the Colored Peoples," he wrote. It did occur to him that the natives had first banded together, struck out, and then drove the aid away. But who could trust poorly trained native journalists to keep events in order?

The researcher had done a study at home of the Afro-Brazilian personality that had won him a university chair and accolades from people that mattered. But jealous colleagues had written scathing critiques of the book, challenging him to evaluate his profile of the African, Indian, and Latin character in light of what had emerged in revolutionary Cuba.

"Could be, my friend, that you've confused the coping mechanisms of the oppressed with racial character," Professor Amado had said over sherry. The snide remark of other most esteemed colleagues still ringing in his ears now left him stinging in his clothes despite the cold wind chafing his neck.

"Dependency Complex," he underlined twice, slicing through the index cards he used for notes. Fatalistic, lazy, irresponsible, no sense of time. It was true throughout the colored world. It explained those people's condition of poverty.

Rows of dark, sleepy faces swam before his eyes: the dock workers he had interviewed, the fisherfolk, the beggars, the servants at his in-laws' estate, the vagabonds in the cities. He examined the faces, the postures, the mien of passengers on board, tucking his feet under the bench as the woman with the blowing hair ushered the little girl past. "Fed, then abandoned, birds and people will attack," he wrote, planning his next book and his counter-remarks for the most esteemed Professor Amado.

The mother led the girl back to their seats, the passengers along the way grabbing the small hand and leading the child to the next hand outstretched. The mother kept her head down, waiting for the brown leather shoes that marked their places next. She sat, her unbound hair hard to gather up with the wind sweeping under the tin roofing. The little girl raised up on her knees and caught up the billowing hair in bunches, and the mother secured it at last with the wire.

The gentleman in brown shoes kept his eyes all the while averted, tried not to notice when the hair blew all over his shoulder and chest, giving him a wayward beard. He stared up at the corrugated tin roofing so like the poorer houses in his district. Tin sheets held together with rusted bolts no longer holding against the wind. Nothing these days was holding against the winds, thinking of his family scattered. One son lost to Coca-Cola and bell-bottoms, hair so long the gentleman was ashamed to call him kin. Another son gone underground and no word sent in years and years. His unmarried sister leaving his household without his permission, dreams of Paris, London, and New York salons taking her off, defying his authority, rejecting the suitor so carefully selected, so carefully groomed by the two families in question. The outraged family invading his home, backing him up against the piles of fashion magazines abandoned by his sister. He with no bride to offer and no face left.

His mealtimes of late explosive scenes, the magazines flung across the room upsetting the bowls and his digestion. White-faced models in Asian fashions asprawl on the floor and his daughter screaming.

"What cannibals," kicking at the faces in the book. "Occidental cadavers draped in the clothing of the dead. The murdered dead. In the skin of the dead. Our dead they murdered, disemboweled, then they stepped into the skins. Look, look," his daughter would demand, bringing the magazines to the table. "Look what they've done to their eyes," jabbing her finger. He no longer said she was a fool to get so upset over Occidentals who chose to draw dark slants on their eyes. It only made her wild. There was no peace in his house any more, no calm. Each day, each meal, his daughter became a hurricane uncontained, blowing his composure apart.

Then his daughter, without his permission, joined the women's union and the women's detachment of the band who called themselves the People's Army. Leaving home each morning to hop a truck with other brazen women to work at the salt flats, or shoot guns in the woods, or pitch manure for the forbidden co-op farms downriver. She would argue with him, shout into his face, call him feudal, fool, collaborator, corrupt. And he would go back into the house breathless. And never once these days did his wife say he was right. She was all but mute and seemingly paralyzed, for she made no move to censure the wild daughter.

The gentleman in brown shoes squinted up at the slits of sky, wondering if the roof would hold or fly off, the bolts no match for the irresistible winds. His authority no match for the hurricane that was his daughter. His sovereignty dissolved like the near-worthless currency he carried strapped around his belly, waterlogged in the money belt, having been stashed in the well, hidden from the soldiers and the people's militia. It had mildewed. And despite the drying by the fire, the money never seemed to recover. He was off to the city now uncomfortable to try to float a loan on damp collateral and rebuild his household. What was to become of him now that his seed was scattered in the winds? Who would manage the land, keep up the line, the traditions? Not the transistor-radio son who stayed in the movie houses now. His wife was far too old for further family. He wondered if indeed he should find a new wife and start again.

The little girl smoothed her mother's hair back from her temples and wondered if the gentleman was tipping away because of the boat's lurching or because of them. She felt a quivering in her mother's body and feared that any minute her mother might bolt from her grasp, thrash about on the deck, pitch herself over the side. At night sometimes, the girl would awaken to her mother's reliving of the torture. Memory surging through her body as she rolled around on the floor, banging down the chairs, doubling up tightly, then springing apart as though taunted by an electric prod, hands tight between her legs protecting what'd been violated.

"Nothing," she'd moan. "I'll tell you nothing," her head jerking as though some unseen hand had her by the hair. "You'll never break our spirits. We cannot be defeated."

"Nothing. I'll tell you nothing . . ." Over and over, louder and louder, thrashing about on the hard-swept dirt floor, flinging away into the walls the women who rushed in from the next hut but could never hold her down and only sometimes could shove a bit of wood between her teeth to keep her from swallowing her own tongue.

"Nothing. I'll tell you nothing." The girl might manage to get her mother's head up off the floor and into her lap. "You'll never break our spirits," soothing the temples. "We cannot be defeated," rocking, rocking.

The little girl continued her brushing and smoothing, wondering if the gentleman could be relied upon if her mother bolted. If she herself didn't panic, she would demand he jump to aid the minute the first words were blurted out. "Nothing. I'll tell you nothing." It would take nimble timing, for often the bourgeoisie would not touch the miserable shoeless. "You'll never break our spirit." But then the engine was switched off and her mother relaxed, looking over the side, her face full in the wind. "We cannot be defeated." It had been the vibrations of the boat, the girl concluded, that had made her mother shiver. It had been the lurching of rough waters that had tipped the gentlemen away from them.

The mother grasped her daughter's hand and avoided looking just yet at the gathering on the landing. She watched instead the women pounding clothes on the rocks, shooing mud hens from the wash, chasing the pigs from the soap. Workers from the textile plant farther down were spreading strips of newly dyed cloth across the grass to dry. Around tents of mosquito netting humped over bamboo poles, women and young girls moved in a circle, stitching up the hems, moving round and round as in the country dances of old. Closer by, some workers round the braziers huddled, coaxing brochettes and threading wild onions and hunks of mud hens on twigs while an old woman at a separate fire watched the rice boil up.

Rising slowly, the mother wound a bit of cloth into a coil for her head. The gentleman helped her hoist the bundles onto the coil, stepping back fast when their hands touched in her hair. The deck shivered violently when the lower ramp clanked down, and she lost her balance against his body that was there then wasn't there. She held her daughter's shoulder as the oxen loped off from the deck below, cyclists weaving in and out among the porters unloading crates and sacks and the sticky black boxes that caused murmurs, the trucks sputtering in the wet sand then honking people out of the way. When the top ramp banged down, she steadied herself against her daughter, and they followed the soldier off; he then quickly joined a group of uniformed men by a cement bunker from a war before.

The taxi driver rushed forward to grab the American's luggage. He wrestled the handbags from the Frenchwoman, collared everybody in shoes. Gabbing loudly in snatches of this language and that, he loaded suitcases onto his humpback taxi, stuffing, jamming the bags into the rack. He ticked off the meter in his mind, not sure just yet how to stuff and jam the owners of the luggage into the car. Once more he brushed by the weighted-down woman and the stumbling girl to check the suspicious-looking young man with the hard brown face. There was something about him, a look he had seen before. A look that could mean money. He studied the young man's tracks in the sand, and his meter jumped. Rubber treads from downed American planes. Ho Chi Minh sandals. Just in from the border. Tall, brown, thin, hard, thirty or so. Someone might pay plenty even in the dwindling market these days of revolution. The driver crowded five into his humpback taxi and sped off, already peddling the information in his mind.

A young boy with a wheelbarrow had been studying the passengers, on the watch for shoes with big heels that could mean smuggling and might mean a meal for him, on watch for baskets with false bottoms that might mean new clothes for him if the tip paid off. He wheeled among the the workers gathered at the landing for news of the downriver districts, just as he daily wheeled among the civil servants gathered at the airport for news of the world. Other people on the landing were there to greet relatives, come to squeeze into already over-crowded rooms in the city.

No shoes or baskets worth noting, the barrow boy shifted his attention to the squat woman in the straw hat who seemed to be waiting for the crowd to disperse before approaching the woman with the bundle on her head and the little girl over-loaded with smaller bundles. He recognized the squat woman in the conical hat. She worked at the Imperial Palace, which some joked would be called the People's Palace soon. She shined shoes in the arcade, boiled sheets out back, served coffee in the rooms, and seemed to be ever out walking—no doubt involved in something clandestine, something worth uncover-ing. Rebel or paid informer, he hadn't decided. He had been told to simply keep his eyes open.

He watched the two women meet and speak. The squat one using her straw hat to fan then shield the other from the sun. The boy wheeled his barrow in closer, for they would be need-ing him for the bundles. The wind blew their words the other way, so he moved in closer still and begin loading up.

"a good girl   used to hard work . . ."

"in good hands   don't worry   will not be abused . . ."

"a permit for my husband's release   soon the family will be reunited   Can you find room for our things?"

"Soon the country will be free," the squat woman was say-ing, looking directly into his mouth. "Then we'll all be reu-nited."

"news of your son   alive though sickly   consumption damp cells and   and your baby?"

"Dead."

The barrow boy awaited instructions, looking from the mother to the girl to the squat woman from the Imperial Palace Hotel.

The mother bent and embraced her daughter, then quickly turned and trotted back up the boat ramp. For a moment the girl felt the breeze from her mother's leave-taking more strongly than the currents off the bay. But soon the wind picked up again as the boat eased out. The wind weighted with soap from the washerwomen was heavy on her, enclasping her, jamming up her nose.

At the precinct bunker, they'd stuffed hoses up her nose and pumped in soapy water, fish brine, water from the district's sewer till her belly swelled up, bloated to near bursting. Then they beat her with the poles, sticks, rods of bamboo, some iron till she vomited, nearly drowning. She told them nothing. Heard none of their questions, her own prayers too loud in her ears to hear anything but her own hopes that her brothers did not betray the cadres in the cellars, in the temples, in the woods.

Coming to on a ribbed floor, the door of the metal cage swung wide and the moon spilling in, she smelled the soap again on the uniform of the man in boots who told her her brothers had been freed. She smelled the soap on him and could not move, had to be shoved past the bamboo fence and iron barbs. He had stuffed a pack of food into her arms clutched round her belly. A pack of food wrapped in plantain leaves and elephant ears. A pack she clutched unnoticed all the way home and all the way to the temple, then all the way to the jetty.

Of course she had expected the sea birds to drop down poisoned into the waters. Had not thought they'd live through the food long enough to attack her. She had been caught off-guard so preoccupied, thinking about the soldier in his boots who'd set her free and given her perfectly good food, as it turned out. And pitying him. For what shame would overwhelm him when he reexperienced his natural self and knew once more right from wrong. But that, the elders had taught her in the spring, was the wonderful thing about revolution. It gave one a chance to amend past crimes, to change, to be human. And that is why, the elders had taught her in the rainy season, the youth were so important, for they would prove to the ancestors that it had not been foolish to fight for the right to be free, to be human. And that was why, the elders had taught her in the first crop season, that she herself mattered, that what she did or did not do would matter for the yet unborn. So in winter when they took her from the schoolhouse and dragged her off for interrogation, she was already an elder in her mind.

The woman from the Imperial Palace walked just behind the barrow boy, looking sadly at his grimy, spare body, wondering who had recruited him and for what, but had not fed him. She took the little girl's hand as she'd been doing for so long, training the youth for the Front. Wondering how she'd look in her vendor apron stationed at the embassies, in the market, at the Exchange, in the hotel lobbies hawking combs, acting as guide, securing information about troop movements. The woman from the hotel tried to keep her mind on the work at hand and the days ahead as the cadres prepared for the liberation of the city. Tried not to fret over the sickly barrow boy with the swollen hands. He may not have a mother, she was thinking, but he certainly has a future.

The barrow boy stole a glance at the girl and the squat woman walking hand in hand at his side now, just one or two paces behind him, so close he knew they could hear him groaning. It wasn't the weight of the barrow that hurt, but the grasping of the handles that shot pain up his arms, down his legs, scattered through his body, lodging hot up under his tongue. He shoved ahead, staring at his greenish puffy hands, wishing instead he walked between them, clasping theirs.

THE
LONG
NIGHT

It whistled past her, ricocheted off the metal hamper and slammed into the radiator pipe, banging the door ajar. Glass was crashing in the apartment below, taking a long time finishing, as though happening in a slow-motion filming. Spatters of concrete and brick nearby, splintering of wood. The ping of a bullet on the fire escape. Storms of grit heaved up against the livingroom windows. Herds over the roof, bellowing. And something else. Pots and pans maybe, or cymbals as though dropped from two thousand stories. Out back somewhere a car stalling, coughing, sputtering, then, like the garbage cans being scraped against concrete, turning over.

"Don't kill 'em. Don't kill—" A barrage of shots and a radio suddenly up then mute.

She sat huddled in the dark, balled up tight, deep within the bathtub. Her hands were bleeding where the nails cut, fists as clenched as teeth, as mercilessly drawing blood. Her eyes fixed

94

on the fissure in the porcelain just below the faucet, a split leading down to the drain.

My lifeline. She opened her mouth to say it. The dark flooded in, but nothing came out. *I'll never,* she thought, *I'll never take another bath in this tub again. If I get through the night,* she added. *If I . . .*

Many wouldn't. Many hadn't. A student on the stoop still where death at eight o'clock had seeped into a hole in the back of his neck.

Heavy thuds on the stairs coming two, three, five steps at a time. Bells ringing. Bodies heaving against doors. She slammed her face shut and squashed herself into, under the faucet, down the drain.

"A mop and pail, for chrissakes!"

A door slamming with difficulty, meeting resistance. Banging. Bolts. "Go away. Please, please go away. We got lil kids in here. Please."

Heavy boots on the steps again. A menace on the landing. Grunt breathing at her door. A sudden body crash against the steel plating, wood, locks. She jammed her mouth down between her knees to keep from laughing or screaming, one. *A police lock to lock the police out.* Down the hall another weight against a door. Someone crying. Near the stair hushed growling.

"Shoot the lock off . . . gotta . . . mop . . . pail . . . so much blood."

"Suppose someone's home? We don't want . . ."

"What'll we charge em with?"

"Think of somethin' . . . riot soon."

"Maybe . . . hate to get caught up here . . . take your badge off."

In the Schenley box marked This Side Up a cargo too precious to destroy, dangerous to transport, death to surrender up. If she dashed to the kitchen and skidded under the table, there might be time to. *To what? Why think of it now,* she thought, crushing herself closer to the drain and imagining instead her limbs scooting across the rooftops, broken field running over the skylights, past pipes like Carl had taught her, the leap to 417, then down two flights, the closet with the false wall, the black room they'd built. She'd wallpapered the closet herself, tap-tapping to be sure of a uniform sound. Wallpapered all the closets with the same quaint, floral pattern Carl's mother had sent all the way from Montreal.

"Open up. Police."

Wanted: The Killers of Lester Long/The Killers of Bobby Hutton/The Killers of James Rutledge/The Killers of Teddy—

"Open up in there."

Do Not Embrace Amnesia. The Struggle Continues. Memory Is a Powerful—

"Shoot the fuckin' lock off, for chrissakes."

The Assault on the Begone Pesticide Plant Was an Assault on Guinea Pigism in Our Community. The People Spoke. The Attack on the Precinct Was an Attack on Lawlessness. The People—

A blast. Another. The door shoved brutally back against the carpet she'd never laid quite right.

Harriet Tubman's Work Must Continue. Support the—

And if I'm caught. She dared not think it. Caught in a bathtub. No place to flee but down. And they'd hound her into the pipes. The savage claw scratching against metal, clutching for flesh. *The box:* posters, photos, statistics . . . *all that work. Is the tablecloth long enough?* She pictured it somewhere behind her left eye where a throb had begun. *The box.* The addresses were under the camphor bar in the silverware drawer. Detective special, stolen from ballistics in the back coils of the refrigerator in a rat-poison box. In the sugar cannister the negatives of the campus agents. And in the safest place, tacked to the cork board in clear view, the number you called which for fifty dollars taped to a page of the main library encyclopedia yielded up a copy of your dossier. Fifty feet of useless footage sprang from her eye sprockets: hurtling herself through the dark to the kitchen with a torch. Or running full tilt at the ransackers with a lance.

"Get the light."

"Shithead, we'll draw our own fire. Flashlight."

"Where's the kitchen in this place?"

They'd tracked in a smell. It filled the rooms. It sought her out and gagged her. They'd find the box. *Africa Supports Us. Asia Supports Us. Latin Ameri*—

"Get the mop there."

The PRG Supports Us. The FLQ Supports Us. The FLN—

"No pail. Look for some bucket . . ."

They'll find the box. They'll look for me. The blows. The madness. The best of myself splattered bright against the porcelain. No. The best of myself inviolate. Maybe.

They'd ask about the others. Cracking her head against the faucet, they'd demand something ungivable, but settle perhaps for anything snatchable, any anything to sanctify the massacre in the streets below. And would she allow them to tear the best of herself from herself, blast her from her place, that place inviolate, make her heap ratfilth into that place, that place where no corruption touched, where she curled up and got cozy or spread her life leisurely out for inventory. Hurtle her into the yellow-green slime of her own doing, undoing, to crawl on wrecked limbs in that violated place, that place. Could she trust herself. Was she who she'd struggled to become so long. To become in an obscene instant the exact who she'd always despised, condemned to that place, fouled.

She would tell. They would beat her and she would tell more. They would taunt and torture and she would tell all. They'd put a gun in her eye and she would tell even what there wasn't to tell. Chant it. Sing it. Moan it. Shout it. Incriminate her neighbors. Sell her mama. Hawk her daddy. Trade her friends. Turn in everybody. Turn on everything. And never be the same. Dead or alive, never be the same. Blasted from her place.

My children will . . . but then I'll have no children, there'll be no room in that place to incubate children. They'd know. Growing there in the folds of that fouled place they'd know. And they'd ask. And their eyes would wipe me out.

"What's this?"

Rummaging in the refrigerator. Something sloshing to the floor. The ten-watt floodlight.

"Just get some papers to wipe our . . . look at my shoes."

Faucet running. Glasses slipping off the drain to crash against the pots.

"My God, my boots are full of blood . . ."

". . . footprints . . ."

My ancestors. Those breaths around me in sudden inexplicable moments of yes; welcome intrusions from some other where saying, yes, keep on. . . . They'll spit on me in the night.

"Let's get out of here."

Could she tell? Wouldn't her heart vault into the brain and stomp it out? Trained. In case of betrayal, self-destruct.

The bathroom door flung wide and a gust blew over her neck and back. That smell. A glob of light tumbled round the dark and settled somewhere. She could not look. Maybe she was the light. Balled up so tight, so hot in panic, so near death and another death yet, glowin', glowin' red/orange/yellow, glinting shots of shine around the arena in a suicidal beam. She would not look up. She would not look and meet those eyes. The eyes of the beast. Of the golden monkey that spits and kills.

"Here's a bucket."

The scrape of the bucket being dragged out from behind the toilet—scraping across her spine. The voice a boot on her neck. This was it, and what did she have. Heat behind the refrigerator. Heat in the Kotex box in the back of the linen closet. And she in the bathtub. With that smell. That reek that stopped her heart and forced her eyelids up. And then she saw him. Up too close to the screen, surreal. Jello-like around the edges like Superman taking off. Superman leaping into the bathtub to break her back. *No.* She would never tell. Strike. She would strike. Someone or three would go down in the go-down.

She'd made out a will. They all had. Long line of relatives and associates named executors of estate in case of funnytime death. Statutes of limitations had a way of running out when charges were brought against the police.

"Let's go."

The glob of light clicked off. The drip of the toilet splashing onto the tiles now. Door pulled in starts and stops shut. The heavy crashing thuds down the stairs. She listened. Tight up against the lifeline fissure of rust gone green, she swept the mind clean to hear the footfalls, to isolate them. Someone had stayed behind. Someone was waiting in the dark. Sly death crouched to pounce upon her life and wreck it. Crouched and waiting, impatient to tear her with savage teeth, her essence spilling out of place and oozing down the chin, the chest, the arm. Impatient he would creep across the carpet of leaves that covered the pit. And she would strike. She was poised for the attack. And with what would she undo him? A can of Ajax? A wire soap dish? *My Afro pick,* she decided, spotting it on the toilet tank. Seemed fitting. She almost wished someone were there. Silence. Stuck horns, screaming, scurrying of feet against the slush, but silence. Riffling of pages somewhere in the living room. Curtains fluttering in shreds. But silence.

Vibrations from the porcelain were drowsing her asleep. Not the same vibes as from other walls.

Drafts from school walls blew rudely in the young face awaking, as she stood in the corner under punishment from those early caretakers. Chill breeze quivering the nostril hairs where up against the wall the cast of twelve, assembled for some droll Punch and Judy show, awaited directions from those other caretakers. Or the accurately known vibrations from walls encountered deliberately blindfolded, when they learned to maneuver in the dark, to touchtalk pipes and rods out of their hiding places and assemble guns and radio sets by Braille. Trained to recognize obstacles by the length and chill of their breezes, so as not to bump and knock breath and blood out and leave a break in the chain, a hole in the network, a chink just large enough for a boot to kick through, a butt to muzzle in. The walls of the bathtub were different.

More like the vibes of the stone quarry of two summers before where she and Carl had worked for $1.10 an hour for the privilege of talking with workers who worked for $1.10 an hour for the privilege of eating. Or like the walls of the grotto where she'd spent the only vacation of her life, wet, love-warmed and dazzled for a whole summer with Carl. Shouting foolishness in all the tongues of the sea, they swam underwater entangling four legs and surfacing, felt/heard their shouts glanceback off the grotto walls cool and hollow against their cheeks. That was last summer. The Carl of moss and fruit and bitten shoulders and the privacy of mosquito-net tents. The Carl before the call to Canada. The call into exile.

She stopped shivering at first light. That milk-of-magnesia-bottle blue, Carl had said. She looked at her hands, sticky and brown, pieces of nail like glass shards atop a brick wall. Pain shot straight through. Like in the days of intensive training when the hands would no longer open and shut by ordinary means. Hot water, Ben-Gay, the gun strapped in the hand with adhesive tape. The practice shots squeezed off, bringing tears down the nose on the inside, then pushed back again by the smoke. Chinese mustard, Carl had said.

It took all of ten minutes to wrap the hands around the edge of the tub and hoist herself up. That same tremor of hysterical laughter, stopped before, now erupted from her knees it seemed. Straddling a bathtub, a bucking-bronco bathtub, she could not stop it now. Lava poured from her mouth and flopped her head over onto the hamper, denting it while the lower half of her body was still being dragged up out of the tub like some crazed water creature pushing for the next stage.

"Oh my," she guffawed, like Carl's mother used to when Carl broke through her ladylike decorum with some wild tale. *Oh my, she'd said when she'd opened her door to find Carl's woman there and Carl already gone. Oh my, when Concordia Bridge flashed on the screen, fixing them in the middle of the rug. The tan station wagon speeding past the police barriers, a mere blur between television cameras, barely visible through snow and distance as it seemingly flew onto the island where the Cuban officials waited with the plane. She had dropped her bag on the rug and run to the television, the older woman already there turning up the sound.*

They'd traded the lives of two Canadian trade commissioners for the release of the West Indian students charged with kidnapping a dean, extortion, and untold damage to the university's two-million-dollar computer complex. For their release and safe passage to Algeria for the students and what was left of the cell. And she had come too late. Aboard the plane she'd learned that Algeria had refused them. In the cab, she'd heard a West Indian diplomat disinherit the fugitives. She had arrived at Carl's mother's in time for the televised getaway and little more.

Buzzy, Hassan, and Lydia barely being picked up by the cameras as they got out of the station wagon. The other Bloods she didn't know, mere coattails heading into a building. Then Carl, barely recognizable through the swirling snow, waving his last goodbye, as his mother patted the TV box as though it were only a photograph she was seeing safely souvenired in a snowball paperweight.

She was was out of the tub now, slipping unsteadily. She'd thought she'd stand upright. That was the idea. But she found herself lunging toward the pockmarked windows like a stumble drunk. One rectangle of bullet-splattered frame led to the pavement below, where she wanted to be. But not like this, in a faint, leaning onto the fire escape slats in a swoon. But she did want to be below.

For the people would be emerging from the dark of their places. Surfacing for the first time in eons into clarity. And their skins would shrink from—not remembering it like this— the climate. Feet wary of the pavement for heartless jokes they did remember. And their brains, true to their tropism, would stretch the whole body up to the light, generating new food out of the old staple wisdoms. And they would look at each other as if for the first time and wonder, who is this one and that one. And she would join the circle gathered round the ancient stains in the street. And someone would whisper, and who are you. And who are you. And who are we. And they would tell each other in a language that had evolved, not by magic, in the caves.

Medley

I could tell the minute I got in the door and dropped my bag, I wasn't staying. Dishes piled sky-high in the sink looking like some circus act. Glasses all ghosty on the counter. Busted tea bags, curling canteloupe rinds, white cartoons from the Chinamen, green sacks from the deli, and that damn dog creeping up on me for me to wrassle his head or kick him in the ribs one. No, I definitely wasn't staying. Couldn't even figure why I'd come. But picked my way to the hallway anyway till the laundry-stuffed pillowcases stopped me. Larry's bass blocking the view to the bedroom.

"That you, Sweet Pea?"

"No, man, ain't me at all," I say, working my way back to the suitcase and shoving that damn dog out the way. "See ya round," I holler, the door slamming behind me, cutting off the words abrupt.

*   *   *

Quite naturally sitting cross-legged at the club, I embroider a little on the homecoming tale, what with an audience of two crazy women and a fresh bottle of Jack Daniels. Got so I could actually see shonuff toadstools growing in the sink. Canteloupe seeds sprouting in the muck. A goddamn compost heap breeding near the stove, garbage gardens on the grill.

"Sweet Pea, you oughta hush, cause you can't possibly keep on lying so," Pot Limit's screaming, tears popping from her eyes. "Lawd hold my legs, cause this liar bout to kill me off."

"Never mind about Larry's housekeeping, girl," Sylvia's soothing me, sloshing perfectly good bourbon all over the table. "You can come and stay with me till your house comes through. It'll be like old times at Aunt Merriam's."

I ease back into the booth to wait for the next set. The drummer's fooling with the equipment, tapping the mikes, hoping he's watched, so I watch him. But feeling worried in my mind about Larry, cause I've been through days like that myself. Cold cream caked on my face from the day before, hair matted, bathrobe funky, not a clean pair of drawers to my name. Even the emergency ones, the draggy cotton numbers stuffed way in the back of the drawer under the scented paper gone. And no clean silverware in the box and the last of the paper cups gone too. Icebox empty cept for a rock of cheese and the lone water jug that ain't even half full that's how anyhow the thing's gone on. And not a clue as to the next step. But then Pot Limit'll come bamming on the door to say So-and-so's in town and can she have the card table for a game. Or Sylvia'll send a funny card inviting herself to dinner and even giving me the menu. Then I zoom through that house like a manic work brigade till me and the place ready for white-glove inspection. But what if some somebody or other don't intervene for Larry, I'm thinking.

The drummer's messin round on the cymbals, head cocked

to the side, rings sparkling. The other dudes are stepping out from behind the curtain. The piano man playing with the wah-wah doing splashy, breathy science fiction stuff. Sylvia checking me out to make sure I ain't too blue. Blue got hold to me, but I lean foward out of the shadows and babble something about how off the bourbon tastes these days. Hate worryin Sylvia, who is the kind of friend who bleeds at the eyes with your pain. I drain my glass and hum along with the opening riff of the guitar and I keep my eyes strictly off the bass player, whoever he is.

Larry Landers looked more like a bass player than ole Mingus himself. Got these long arms that drape down over the bass like they were grown special for that purpose. Fine, strong hands with long fingers and muscular knuckles, the dimples deep black at the joints. His calluses so other-colored and hard, looked like Larry had swiped his grandmother's tarnished thimbles to play with. He'd move in on that bass like he was going to hump it or something, slide up behind it as he lifted it from the rug, all slinky. He'd become one with the wood. Head dipped down sideways bobbing out the rhythm, feet tapping, legs jiggling, he'd look good. Thing about it, though, ole Larry couldn't play for shit. Couldn't never find the right placement for the notes. Never plucking with enough strength, despite the perfectly capable hands. Either you didn't hear him at all or what you heard was off. The man couldn't play for nuthin is what I'm saying. But Larry Landers was baad in the shower, though.

He'd soap me up and down with them great, fine hands, doing a deep bass walking in the back of his mouth. And I'd just have to sing, though I can't sing to save my life. But we'd have one hellafyin musical time in the shower, lemme tell you. "Green Dolphin Street" never sounded like nuthin till Larry bopped out them changes and actually made me sound good.

On "My Funny Valentine" he'd do a whizzing sounding bow thing that made his throat vibrate real sexy and I'd cutesy up the introduction, which is, come to think of it, my favorite part. But the main number when the hot water started running out was "I Feel Like Making Love." That was usually the wind up of our repertoire cause you can imagine what that song can do to you in the shower and all.

Got so we spent a helluva lotta time in the shower. Just as well, cause didn't nobody call Larry for gigs. He a nice man, considerate, generous, baad in the shower, and good taste in music. But he just wasn't nobody's bass player. Knew all the stances, though, the postures, the facial expressions, had the choreography down. And right in the middle of supper he'd get some Ron Carter thing going in his head and hop up from the table to go get the bass. Haul that sucker right in the kitchen and do a number in dumb show, all the playing in his throat, the acting with his hands. But that ain't nuthin. I mean that can't get it. I can impersonate Betty Carter if it comes to that. The arms crooked just so, the fingers popping, the body working, the cap and all, the teeth, authentic. But I got sense enough to know I ain't nobody's singer. Actually, I am a mother, though I'm only just now getting it together. And too, I'm an A-1 manicurist.

Me and my cousin Sinbad come North working our show in cathouses at first. Set up a salon right smack in the middle of Miz Maybry's Saturday traffic. But that wasn't no kind of life to be bringing my daughter into. So I parked her at a boarding school till I could make some other kind of life. Wasn't no kind of life for Sinbad either, so we quit.

Our first shop was a three-chair affair on Austin. Had a student barber who could do anything—blow-outs, do's, corn rows, weird cuts, afros, press and curl, whatever you wanted.

Plus he din't gab you to death. And he always brought his sides and didn't blast em neither. He went on to New York and opened his own shop. Was a bootblack too then, an old dude named James Noughton, had a crooked back and worked at the post office at night, and knew everything about everything, read all the time.

"Whatcha want to know about Marcus Garvey, Sweet Pea?"

If it wasn't Garvey, it was the rackets or the trucking industry or the flora and fauna of Greenland or the planets or how the special effects in the disaster movies were done. One Saturday I asked him to tell me about the war, cause my nephew'd been drafted and it all seemed so wrong to me, our men over there in Nam fighting folks who fighting for the same things we are, to get that blood-sucker off our backs.

Well, what I say that for. Old dude gave us a deep knee bend, straight up eight-credit dissertation on World Wars I and II—the archduke getting offed, Africa cut up like so much cake, Churchill and his cigars, Gabriel Heatter on the radio, Hitler at the Olympics igging Owens, Red Cross doing Bloods dirty refusing donuts and bandages, A. Philip Randolph scaring the white folks to death, Mary McLeod Bethune at the White House, Liberty Bond drives, the Russian front, frostbite of the feet, the Jew stiffs, the gypsies no one mourned . . . the whole johnson. Talked straight through the day, Miz Mary's fish dinner growing cold on the radiator, his one and only customer walking off with one dull shoe. Fell out exhausted, his shoe rag limp in his lap, one arm draped over the left foot platform, the other clutching his heart. Took Sinbad and our cousin Pepper to get the old man home. I stayed with him all night with the ice pack and a fifth of Old Crow. He liked to die.

After while trade picked up and with a better class of folk too. Then me and Sinbad moved to North and Gaylord and called the shop Chez Sinbad. No more winos stumbling in or deadbeats wasting my time talking raunchy shit. The paperboy, the numbers man, the dudes with classier hot stuff coming in on Tuesday mornings only. We did up the place nice. Light globes from a New Orleans whorehouse, Sinbad likes to lie. Brown-and-black-and-silver-striped wallpaper. Lots of mirrors and hanging plants. Them old barber chairs spruced up and called antiques and damn if someone didn't buy one off us for eight hundred, cracked me up.

I cut my schedule down to ten hours in the shop so I could do private sessions with the gamblers and other business men and women who don't like sitting around the shop even though it's comfy, specially my part. Got me a cigar showcase with a marble top for serving coffee in clear glass mugs with heatproof handles too. My ten hours in the shop are spent leisurely. And my twenty hours out are making me a mint. Takes dust to be a mother, don't you know.

It was a perfect schedule once Larry Landers came into my life. He part-timed at a record shop and bartended at Topp's on the days and nights I worked at the shops. That gave us most of Monday and Wednesdays to listen to sides and hit the clubs. Gave me Fridays all to myself to study in the library and wade through them college bulletins and get to the museum and generally chart out a routine for when Debbie and me are a team. Sundays I always drive to Delaware to see her, and Larry detours to D.C. to see his sons. My bankbook started telling me I was soon going to be a full-time mama again and a college girl to boot, if I can ever talk myself into doing a school thing again, old as I am.

Life with Larry was cool. Not just cause he wouldn't hear about me going halves on the bills. But cause he was an easy man to be easy with. He liked talking softly and listening to music. And he liked having folks over for dinner and cards.

Larry a real nice man and I liked him a lot. And I liked his
friend Hector, who lived in the back of the apartment. Ole
moon-face Hector went to school with Larry years ago and is
some kind of kin. And they once failed in the funeral business
together and I guess those stories of them times kinda keep
them friends.

The time they had to put Larry's brother away is their best
story, Hector's story really, since Larry got to play a little grief
music round the edges. They decided to pass up a church
service, since Bam was such a treacherous desperado wouldn't
nobody want to preach over his body and wouldn't nobody
want to come to hear no lies about the dearly departed un-
timely ripped or cut down or whatever. So Hector and Larry
set up some kind of pop stand awning right at the gravesite,
expecting close blood only. But seems the whole town turned
out to make sure ole evil, hell-raising Bam was truly dead.
Dudes straight from the barber chair, the striped ponchos
blowing like wings, fuzz and foam on they face and all, lumber-
ing up the hill to the hole taking bets and talking shit, relating
how Ole Crazy Bam had shot up the town, shot up the jail, shot
up the hospital pursuing some bootlegger who'd come up one
keg short of the order. Women from all around come to demand the lid be lifted so they could check for themselves and
be sure that Bam was stone cold. No matter how I tried I
couldn't think of nobody bad enough to think on when they
told the story of the man I'd never met.

Larry and Hector so bent over laughing bout the funeral, I
couldn't hardly put the events in proper sequence. But I could
surely picture some neighbor lady calling on Larry and Bam's
mama reporting how the whole town had turned out for the
burying. And the mama snatching up the first black thing she
could find to wrap around herself and make an appearance. No
use passing up a scene like that. And Larry prancing round the

kitchen being his mama. And I'm too stunned to laugh, not at somebody's mama, and somebody's brother dead. But him and Hector laughing to beat the band and I can't help myself.

Thing about it, though, the funeral business stories are Hector's stories and he's not what you'd call a good storyteller. He never gives you the names, so you got all these he's and she's floating around. And he don't believe in giving details, so you got to scramble to paint your own pictures. Toward the end of that particular tale of Bam, all I could picture was the townspeople driving a stake through the dead man's heart, then hurling that coffin into the hole right quick. There was also something in that story about the civil rights workers wanting to make a case cause a white cop had cut Bam down. But looked like Hector didn't have a hold to that part of the story, so I just don't know.

Stories are not Hector's long suit. But he is an absolute artist on windows. Ole Moon-Face can wash some windows and make you cry about it too. Makes these smooth little turns out there on that little bitty sill just like he wasn't four stories up without a belt. I'd park myself at the breakfast counter and thread the new curtains on the rods while Hector mixed up the vinegar solution real chef-like. Wring out the rags just so, scrunch up the newspapers into soft wads that make you think of cat's paws. Hector was a cat himself out there on the sill, making these marvelous circles in the glass, rubbing the hardhead spots with a strip of steel wool he had pinned to his overalls.

Hector offered to do my car once. But I put a stop to that after that first time. My windshield so clear and sparkling felt like I was in an accident and heading over the hood, no glass there. But it was a pleasure to have coffee and watch Hector. After while, though, Larry started hinting that the apartment wasn't big enough for four. I agreed, thinking he meant Earl had to go. Come to find Larry meant Hector, which was a real drag. I love to be around people who do whatever it is they do with style and care.

Larry's dog's named Earl P. Jessup Bowers, if you can get ready for that. And I should mention straightaway that I do not like dogs one bit, which is why I was glad when Larry said somebody had to go. Cats are bad enough. Horses are a total drag. By the age of nine I was fed up with all that noble horse this and noble horse that. They got good PR, horses. But I really can't use em. Was a fire once when I was little and some dumb horse almost burnt my daddy up messin around, twisting, snorting, broncing, rearing up, doing everything but comin on out the barn like even the chickens had sense enough to do. I told my daddy to let that horse's ass burn. Horses be as dumb as cows. Cows just don't have good press agents is all.

I used to like cows when I was real little and needed to hug me something bigger than a goldfish. But don't let it rain, the dumbbells'll fall right in a ditch and you break a plow and shout yourself hoarse trying to get them fools to come up out the ditch. Chipmunks I don't mind when I'm at the breakfast counter with my tea and they're on their side of the glass doing Disney things in the yard. Blue jays are law-and-order birds, thoroughly despicable. And there's one prize fool in my Aunt Merriam's yard I will one day surely kill. He tries to "whip whip whippoorwill" like the Indians do in the Fort This or That movies when they're signaling to each other closing in on George Montgomery but don't never get around to wiping that sucker out. But dogs are one of my favorite hatreds. All the time woofing, bolting down their food, slopping water on the newly waxed linoleum, messin with you when you trying to read, chewin on the slippers.

Earl P. Jessup Bowers was an especial drag. But I could put up with Earl when Hector was around. Once Hector was gone and them windows got cloudy and gritty, I was through. Kicked that dog every chance I got. And after thinking what it meant, how the deal went down, place too small for four and it was Hector not Earl—I started moving up my calendar so I could get out of there. I ain't the kind of lady to press no ultimatum on no man. Like "Chose, me or the dog." That's unattractive. Kicking Hector out was too. An insult to me, once I got to thinking on it. Especially since I had carefully explained from jump street to Larry that I got one item on my agenda, making a home for me and my kid. So if anybody should've been given walking papers, should've been me.

Anyway. One day Moody comes waltzing into Chez Sinbad's and tips his hat. He glances at his nails and glances at me. And I figure here is my house in a green corduroy suit. Pot Limit had just read my cards and the jack of diamonds kept coming up on my resource side. Sylvia and me put our heads together and figure it got to be some gambler or hustler who wants his nails done. What other jacks do I know to make my fortune? I'm so positive about Moody, I whip out a postcard from the drawer where I keep the emeries and write my daughter to start packing.

"How much you make a day, Miss Lady?"

"Thursdays are always good for fifty," I lie.

He hands me fifty and glances over at Sinbad, who nods that it's cool. "I'd like my nails done at four-thirty. My place."

"Got a customer at that time, Mr. Moody, and I like to stay reliable. How bout five-twenty?"

He smiles a slow smile and glances at Sinbad, who nods again, everything's cool. "Fine," he says. "And do you think you can manage a shave without cutting a person's throat?"

"Mr. Moody, I don't know you well enough to have just cause. And none of your friends have gotten to me yet with that particular proposition. Can't say what I'm prepared to do in the future, but for now I can surely shave you real careful-like."

Moody smiles again, then turns to Sinbad, who says it's cool and he'll give me the address. This look-nod dialogue burns my ass. That's like when you take a dude to lunch and pay the check and the waiter's standing there with *your* money in his paws asking *the dude* was everything all right and later for *you*. Shit. But I take down Moody's address and let the rest roll off me like so much steaming lava. I start packing up my little alligator case—buffer, batteries, clippers, emeries, massager, sifter, arrowroot and cornstarch, clear sealer, magnifying glass, and my own mixture of green and purple pigments.

"Five-twenty ain't five-twenty-one, is it, Miss Lady?"

"Not in my book," I say, swinging my appointment book around so he can see how full it is and how neatly the times are printed in. Course I always fill in phony names case some creep starts pressing me for a session.

For six Thursdays running and two Monday nights, I'm at Moody's bending over them nails with a miner's light strapped to my forehead, the magnifying glass in its stand, nicking just enough of the nails at the sides, tinting just enough with the color so he can mark them cards as he shuffles. Takes an hour to do it proper. Then I sift my talc concoction and brush his hands till they're smooth. Them cards move around so fast in his hands, he can actually tell me he's about to deal from the bottom in the next three moves and I miss it and I'm not new to this. I been a gambler's manicurist for more years than I care to mention. Ten times he'll cut and each time the same fifteen cards in the top cut and each time in exactly the same order. Incredible.

Now, I've known hands. My first husband, for instance. To

see them hands work their show in the grandstands, at a circus, in a parade, the pari-mutuels—artistry in action. We met on the train. As a matter of fact, he was trying to burgle my bag. Some story to tell the grandchildren, hunh? I had to get him straight about robbing from folks. I don't play that. Ya gonna steal, hell, steal back some of them millions we got in escrow is my opinion. We spent three good years on the circuit. Then credit cards moved in. Then choke-and-grab muggers killed the whole tradition. He was reduced to a mere shell of his former self, as they say, and took to putting them hands on me. I try not to think on when things went sour. Try not to think about them big slapping hands, only of them working hands. Moody's working hands were something like that, but even better. So I'm impressed and he's impressed. And he pays me fifty and tips me fifty and shuts up when I shave him and keeps his hands off my lovely person.

I'm so excited counting up my bread, moving up the calendar, making impulsive calls to Delaware and the two of us squealing over the wire like a coupla fools, that what Larry got to say about all these goings-on just rolls off my back like so much molten lead.

"Well, who be up there while he got his head in your lap and you squeezing his goddamn blackheads?"

"I don't squeeze his goddamn blackheads, Larry, on account of he don't have no goddamn blackheads. I give him a shave, a steam, and an egg-white face mask. And when I'm through, his face is as smooth as his hands."

"I'll bet," Larry says. That makes me mad cause I expect some kind of respect for my work, which is better than just good.

"And he doesn't have his head in my lap. He's got a whole barbershop set up on his solarium."

"His what?" Larry squinting at me, raising the wooden

114

spoon he stirring the spaghetti with, and I raise the knife I'm chopping the onions with. Thing about it, though, he don't laugh. It's funny as hell to me, but Larry got no sense of humor sometimes, which is too bad cause he's a lotta fun when he's laughing and joking.

"It's not a bedroom. He's got this screened-in sun porch where he raises African violets and—"

"Please, Sweet Pea. Why don't you quit? You think I'm dumb?"

"I'm serious. I'm serious and I'm mad cause I ain't got no reason to lie to you whatever was going on, Larry." He turns back to the pot and I continue working on the sauce and I'm pissed off cause this is silly. "He sits in the barber chair and I shave him and give him a manicure."

"What else you be giving him? A man don't be paying a good-looking woman to come to his house and all and don't—"

"Larry, if you had the dough and felt like it, wouldn't you pay Pot Limit to come read your cards? And couldn't you keep your hands to yourself and she a good-looking woman? And couldn't you see yourself paying Sylvia to come and cook for you and no funny stuff, and she's one of the best-looking women in town?"

Larry cooled out fast. My next shot was to bring up the fact that he was insulting my work. Do I go around saying the women who pass up Bill the bartender and come to him are after his joint? No, cause I respect the fact that Larry Landers mixes the best piña coladas this side of Barbados. And he's flashy with the blender and the glasses and the whole show. He's good and I respect that. But he cooled out so fast I didn't have to bring it up. I don't believe in overkill, besides I like to keep some things in reserve. He cooled out so fast I realized he wasn't really jealous. He was just going through one of them obligatory male numbers, all symbolic, no depth.

Like the time this dude came into the shop to talk some trash and Sinbad got his ass on his shoulders, talking about the dude showed no respect for him cause for all he knew I could be Sinbad's woman. And me arguing that since that ain't the case, what's the deal? I mean why get hot over what if if what if ain't. Men are crazy. Now there is Sinbad, my blood cousin who grew up right in the same house like a brother damn near, putting me through simple-ass changes like that. Who's got time for grand opera and comic strips, I'm trying to make a life for me and my kid. But men are like that. Gorillas, if you know what I mean.

Like at Topp's sometimes. I'll drop in to have a drink with Larry when he's on the bar and then I leave. And maybe some dude'll take it in his head to walk me to the car. That's cool. I lay it out right quick that me and Larry are a we and then we take it from there, just two people gassing in the summer breeze and that's just fine. But don't let some other dude holler over something like "Hey, man, can you handle all that? Why don't you step aside, junior, and let a man . . ." and blah-de-da-de-dah. They can be the best of friends or total strangers just kidding around, but right away they two gorillas pounding on their chest, pounding on their chest and talking over my head, yelling over the tops of cars just like I'm not a person with some say-so in the matter. It's a man-to-man ritual that ain't got nothing to do with me. So I just get in my car and take off and leave them to get it on if they've a mind to. They got it.

But if one of the gorillas is a relative, or a friend of mine, or a nice kinda man I got in mind for one of my friends, I will stick around long enough to shout em down and point out that they are some ugly gorillas and are showing no respect for me and therefore owe me an apology. But if they don't fit into one of them categories, I figure it ain't my place to try to develop them so they can make the leap from gorilla to human. If their

116

own mamas and daddies didn't care whether they turned out to be amoebas or catfish or whatever, it ain't my weight. I got my own weight. I'm a mother. So they got it.

Like I use to tell my daughter's daddy, the key to getting along and living with other folks is to keep clear whose weight is whose. His drinking, for instance, was not my weight. And him waking me up in the night for them long, rambling, ninety-proof monologues bout how the whole world's made up of victims, rescuers, and executioners and I'm the dirty bitch cause I ain't rescuing him fast enough to suit him. Then got so I was the executioner, to hear him tell it. I don't say nuthin cause my philosophy of life and death is this—I'll go when the wagon comes, but I ain't going out behind somebody else's shit. I arranged my priorities long ago when I jumped into my woman stride. Some things I'll go off on. Some things I'll hold my silence and wait it out. Some things I just bump off, cause the best solution to some problems is to just abandon them.

But I struggled with Mac, Debbie's daddy. Talked to his family, his church, AA, hid the bottles, threatened the liquor man, left a good job to play nurse, mistress, kitten, buddy. But then he stopped calling me Dahlin and started calling me Mama. I don't play that. I'm my daughter's mama. So I split. Did my best to sweeten them last few months, but I'd been leaving for a long time.

The silliest thing about all of Larry's grumblings back then was Moody had no eyes for me and vice versa. I just like the money. And I like watching him mess around with the cards. He's exquisite, dazzling, stunning shuffling, cutting, marking, dealing from the bottom, the middle, the near top. I ain't never seen nothing like it, and I seen a whole lot. The thing that made me mad, though, and made me know Larry Landers wasn't ready to deal with no woman full grown was the way he kept bringing it up, always talking about what he figured was on Moody's mind, like what's on my mind don't count. So I finally did have to use up my reserves and point out to Larry that he was insulting my work and that I would never dream of accusing him of not being a good bartender, of just being another pretty face, like they say.

"You can't tell me he don't have eyes," he kept saying.

"What about my eyes? Don't my eyes count?" I gave it up after a coupla tries. All I know is, Moody wasn't even thinking about me. I was impressed with his work and needed the trade and vice versa.

One time, for instance, I was doing his hands on the solarium and thought I saw a glint of metal up under his jacket. I rearranged myself in the chair so I could work my elbow in there to see if he was carrying heat. I thought I was being cool about it.

"How bout keeping your tits on your side of the table, Miss Lady."

I would rather he think anything but that. I would rather he think I was clumsy in my work even. "Wasn't about tits, Moody. I was just trying to see if you had a holster on and was too lazy to ask."

"Would have expected you too. You a straight-up, direct kind of person." He opened his jacket away with the heel of his hand, being careful with his nails. I liked that.

"It's not about you," he said quietly, jerking his chin in the direction of the revolver. "Had to transport some money today and forgot to take it off. Sorry."

I gave myself two demerits. One for the tits, the other for setting up a situation where he wound up telling me something about his comings and goings. I'm too old to be making mistakes like that. So I apologized. Then gave myself two stars. He had a good opinion of me and my work. I did an extra-fine job on his hands that day.

118

Medley

Then the house happened. I had been reading the rental ads and For Sale columns for months and looking at some awful, tacky places. Then one Monday me and Sylvia lucked up on this cute little white-brick job up on a hill away from the street. Lots of light and enough room and not too much yard to kill me off. I paid my money down and rushed them papers through. Got back to Larry's place all excited and found him with his mouth all poked out.

Half grumbling, half proposing, he hinted around that we all should live at his place like a family. Only he didn't quite lay it out plain in case of rejection. And I'll tell you something, I wouldn't want to be no man. Must be hard on the heart always having to get out there, setting yourself up to be possibly shot down, approaching the lady, calling, the invitation, the rap. I don't think I could handle it myself unless everybody was just straight up at all times from day one till the end. I didn't answer Larry's nonproposed proposal cause it didn't come clear to me till after dinner. So I just let my silence carry whatever meaning it will. Ain't nuthin too much changed from the first day he came to get me from my Aunt Merriam's place. My agenda is still to make a home for my girl. Marriage just ain't one of the things on my mind no more, not after two. Got no regrets or bad feelings about them husbands neither. Like the poem says, when you're handed a lemon, make lemonade, honey, make lemonade. That's Gwen Brook's motto, that's mine too. You get a lemon, well, just make lemonade.

"Going on the road next week," Moody announces one day through the steam towel. "Like you to travel with me, keep my hands in shape. Keep the women off my neck. Check the dudes at my back. Ain't asking you to carry heat or money or put yourself in no danger. But I could use your help." He pauses and I ease my buns into the chair, staring at the steam curling from the towel.

"Wicked schedule though—Mobile, Birmingham, Sarasota Springs, Jacksonville, then Puerto Rico and back. Can pay you two thousand and expenses. You're good, Miss Lady. You're good and you got good sense. And while I don't believe in nothing but my skill and chance, I gotta say you've brought me luck. You a lucky lady, Miss Lady."

He raises his hands and cracks his knuckles and it's like the talking towel has eyes as well cause damn if he ain't checking his cuticles.

"I'll call you later, Moody," I manage to say, mind reeling. With two thousand I can get my stuff out of storage, and buy Debbie a real nice bedroom set, pay tuition at the college too and start my three-credit-at-a-time grind.

Course I never dreamed the week would be so unnerving, exhausting, constantly on my feet, serving drinks, woofing sisters, trying to distract dudes, keeping track of fifty-leven umpteen goings on. Did have to carry the heat on three occasions and had to do a helluva lotta driving. Plus was most of the time holed up in the hotel room close to the phone. I had pictured myself lazying on the beach in Florida dreaming up cruises around the world with two matching steamer trunks with the drawers and hangers and stuff. I'd pictured traipsing through the casinos in Puerto Rico ordering chicken salad and coffee liqueur and tipping the croupiers with blue chips. Shit no. Was work. And I sure as hell learned how Moody got his name. Got so we didn't even speak, but I kept those hands in shape and his face smooth and placid. And whether he won, lost, broke even, or got wiped out, I don't even know. He gave me my money and took off for New Orleans. That trip liked to kill me.

*   *   *

"You never did say nothing interesting about Moody," Pot Limit says insinuatingly, swinging her legs in from the aisle cause ain't nobody there to snatch so she might as well sit comfortable.

"Yeah, she thought she'd put us off the trail with a rip-roaring tale about Larry's housekeeping."

They slapping five and hunching each other and making a whole lotta noise, spilling Jack Daniels on my turquoise T-straps from Puerto Rico.

"Come on, fess up, Sweet Pea," they crooning. "Did you give him some?"

"Ahhh, yawl bitches are tiresome, you know that?"

"Naaw, naaw," say Sylvia, grabbing my arm. "You can tell us. We wantta know all about the trip, specially the nights." She winks at Pot Limit.

"Tell us about this Moody man and his wonderful hands one more time, cept we want to hear how the hands feeel on the flesh, honey." Pot Limit doing a bump and grind in the chair that almost makes me join in the fun, except I'm worried in my mind about Larry Landers.

Just then the piano player comes by and leans over Sylvia, blowing in her ear. And me and Pot Limit mimic the confectionary goings-on. And just as well, cause there's nothin to tell about Moody. It wasn't a movie after all. And in real life the good-looking gambler's got cards on his mind. Just like I got my child on my mind. Onliest thing to say about the trip is I'm five pounds lighter, not a shade darker, but two thousand closer toward my goal.

"Ease up," Sylvia says, interrupting the piano player to fuss over me. Then the drummer comes by and eases in on Pot Limit. And I ease back into the shadows of the booth to think Larry over.

I'm staring at the entrance half expecting Larry to come into Topps, but it's not his night. Then too, the thing is ended if I'd only know it. Larry the kind of man you're either living with him or you're out. I for one would've liked us to continue, me and Debbie in our place, him and Earl at his. But he got so grumpy the time I said that, I sure wasn't gonna bring it up again. Got grumpy in the shower too, got so he didn't want to wash my back.

But that last night fore I left for Birmingham, we had us one crazy musical time in the shower. I kept trying to lure him into "Maiden Voyage," which I really can't do without back-up, cause I can't sing all them changes. After while he come out from behind his sulk and did a Jon Lucien combination on vocal and bass, alternating the sections, eight bars of singing words, eight bars of singing bass. It was baad. Then he insisted on doing "I Love You More Today Than Yesterday." And we like to break our arches, stomping out the beat against the shower mat.

The bathroom was all steamy and we had the curtains open so we could see the plants and watch the candles burning. I had bought us a big fat cake of sandalwood soap and it was matching them candles scent for scent. Must've been two o'clock in the morning and looked like the hot water would last forever and ever and ever. Larry finally let go of the love songs, which were making me feel kinda funny cause I thought it was understood that I was splitting, just like he'd always made it clear either I was there or nowhere.

Then we hit on a tune I don't even know the name of cept I like to scat and do my thing Larry calls Swahili wailing. He laid down the most intricate weaving, walking, bopping, strutting bottom to my singing I ever heard. It inspired me. Took that melody and went right on out that shower, them candles bout used up, the fatty soap long since abandoned in the dish, our bodies barely visible in the steamed-up mirrors walling his bathroom. Took that melody right on out the room and out of doors and somewhere out this world. Larry changing instruments fast as I'm changing moods, colors. Took an alto solo and gave me a rest, worked an intro up on the piano playing the chords across my back, drove me all up into the high register while he weaved in and out around my head on a flute sounding like them chilly pipes of the Andes. And I was Yma Sumac for one minute there, up there breathing some rare air and losing my mind, I was so high on just sheer music. Music and water, the healthiest things in the world. And that hot water pounding like it was part of the group with a union card and all. And I could tell that if that bass could've fit in the tub, Larry would've dragged that bad boy in there and played the hell out of them soggy strings once and for all.

I dipped way down and reached way back for snatches of Jelly Roll Morton's "Deep Creek Blues" and Larry so painful, so stinging on the bass, could make you cry. Then I'm racing fast through Bessie and all the other Smith singers, Mildred Bailey, Billie and imitators, Betty Roche, Nat King Cole vintage 46, a little Joe Carroll, King Pleasure, some Babs. Found myself pulling lines out of songs I don't even like, but ransacked songs just for the meaningful lines or two cause I realized we were doing more than just making music together, and it had to be said just how things stood.

Then I was off again and lost Larry somewhere down there doing scales, sound like. And he went back to that first supporting line that had drove me up into the Andes. And he stayed there waiting for me to return and do some more Swahili wailing. But I was elsewhere and liked it out there and ignored the fact that he was aiming for a wind-up of "I Love You More Today Than Yesterday." I sang myself out till all I could ever have left in life was "Brown Baby" to sing to my little girl.

Larry stayed on the ground with the same supporting line, and the hot water started getting funny and I knew my time was up. So I came crashing down, jarring the song out of shape, diving back into the melody line and somehow, not even knowing what song each other was doing, we finished up together just as the water turned cold.

A
TENdER
MAN

The girl was sitting in the booth, one leg wrapped around the other cartoon-like. Knee socks drooping, panties peeping from her handbag, ears straining from her head for the soft crepe footfalls, straining less Aisha silent and sudden catch her unawares with the dirty news.

She hadn't caught Cliff's attention. His eyes were simply at rest in that direction. And nothing better to do, he had designed a drama of her. His eyes resting on that booth, on that swivel chair, waiting for Aisha to return and fill it. When the chatty woman in the raincoat had been sitting where the nervous girl sat now, Aisha had flashed him a five-minute sign. That was fifteen minutes ago.

He hadn't known he'd mind the waiting. But he'd been feeling preoccupied of late, off-center, anxious even. Thought he could shrug it off, whatever it was. But sitting on the narrow folding chair waiting, nothing to arrest his attention and focus him, he felt crowded by something too heavy to shrug off. He

125

decided he was simply nervous about the impending student takeover.

He flipped through a tattered *Ebony*, pausing at pictures of children, mothers and children, couples and children, grandparents and children. But no father and child. It was a conspiracy, he chuckled to himself, to keep fathers—he searched for a word—outside. He flipped through the eligible bachelors of the year, halting for a long time at the photo of Carl Davis, his ole army mate who'd nearly deserted in the spring of '61. He was now with RCA making $20,000 a year. Cliff wondered doing what.

The girl was picking her face, now close to panic. In a moment she would bolt for the door. He could imagine heads lifting, swiveling, perfect strangers providing each other with hairy explanations. He could hear the women tsk-tsking, certain that their daughters would never. Aisha came through the swinging doors and he relaxed, not realizing till that moment how far he had slipped into the girl's drama. Aisha shot three fingers in his direction and he nodded. The girl was curled up tight now, Cliff felt her tension, staring at the glass slide Aisha slid onto the table. She leaned over the manila folder Aisha opened, hand screening the side of her face as though to block the people out. She was crying. The sobbing audible, though muffled now that the screening hand was doubled up in her mouth. Cliff was uncomfortable amongst so many women and this young one crying. Cliff got up to look for the water fountain.

Up and down the corridors folks walked distractedly, clutching slips of colored papers. A few looked terror-struck, like models for the covers of the books he often found his students buried in. Glancing at the slips of green or white, checking them against the signs on the doors, each had a particular style with the entrance, he noted. Knocking timidly, shivering, Judgment Day. Turning knobs stealthily and looking about, second-story types. Brisk entrances with caps yanked low, yawl deal with me, shit. Cliff moved in and out among the paper-slip clutchers, doorway handlers, teen-agers pulling younger brothers and sisters along, older folk pausing to read the posters. The walls were lined with posters urging VD tests, Pap smears, examinations painless and confidential. In less strident Technicolor, others argued the joys of planned parenthood.

Cliff approached the information desk, for the sister on the switchboard seemed to be wearing two wigs at once and he had to see that. The guard leaned way back before considering his question about the water fountain, stepped away from a woman leaning over the desk inquiring after a clinic, gave wide berth to all the folk who entered and headed in that direction, then pointed out the water fountain, backed up against the desk in a dramatic recoil. Cliff smiled at first and considered fucking with the dude, touching him, maybe drooling a bit on his uniform. But he moved off, feeling unclean.

At the water fountain a young father hoisted his daughter too far into the spout. Cliff held the button down and the brother smiled relief, a two-handed grip centering now the little girl, who gurgled and horsed around in the water, then held a jaw full even after she was put down on the floor again.

"This place is a bitch, ain't it?" The brother nodding vigorous agreement to his own remark.

"My wife's visiting her folks and I'm about to lose my mind with these kids." He smiled proudly, though, jutting his chin in the direction of the rest of his family. Two husky boys around eight and ten were doing base slides in the upper corridor.

"Man, if I had the clap, I sure as hell wouldn't come here for no treatments." His frown made Cliff look around. In that moment the lights seem to dim, the paint job age, the posters slump. A young girl played hopscotch in the litter, her mother pushing her along impatiently.

Yeh, a bitch, Cliff had meant to say, but all that came out was a wheezy mumble.

"My ole lady says to me 'go to the clinic and pick up my pills.' Even calls me long distance to remind me she's running out. 'Don't forget to get the pills, B.J.' So I come to get the damn pills, right?" He ran his hand through his bush, gripping a fistful and tossing his head back and forth. "Man oh man," he groaned, shaking his head by the hair. The gesture had started out as a simple self-caress, had moved swiftly into an I-don't-believe-this-shit nod, and before Cliff knew it, the bro-ther'd become some precinct victim, his head bam-bam against the walls. "Man oh man, this crazy-ass place! Can't even get a word in for the 'What's your clinic number?' 'Where's your card?' 'Have you seen the cashier?' 'Have you got insurance?' 'Are you on the welfare?' 'Do you have a yellow slip?' 'Where's your card?' 'Who's ya mama?' Phwweeoo! I'm goin straight to the drugstore and get me a crate of rubbers right on. I ain't puttin my woman through this shit."

"Daddy." The little girl was yanking on his pants leg for attention. When she got it, she made a big X in the air.

"Oh, right. I forgot. Sorry, baby." He turned to Cliff and shrugged in mock sheepishness. "Gotta watch ya mouth round these kids these days, they get on ya. Stay on my case bout the smoking, can't even bring a poke chop in the house, gotta sneak a can of beer and step out on the fire escape to smoke the dope. Man, these kids somethin!" He was starting that vigorous nodding again, watching his sons approach. Cliff couldn't keep his eyes off the brother's bobbing head. It re-minded him of Granddaddy Mobley so long ago, playing horsy, whinnying down the hallway of Miss Hazel's boardinghouse, that head going a mile a minute and his sister Alma riding high, whipping her horse around the head and shoulders and laughing so hard Miss Hazel threatened to put them out.

"Yeh," he was sighing, nudging Cliff less he miss the chance to dig on the two young dudes coming, punching invisible catcher's mitts, diddyboppin like their daddy must've done it years before. "Later for them pills, anyway. It's back to good ole reliable Trojans."

"Pills dangerous," Cliff said.

"Man, just living is a danger. And every day. Every day, man."

"We going to the poolroom now?" the older boy was asking, nodding first to Cliff.

"I want some Chinese food." The younger seemed to be addressing this to Cliff, shifting his gaze to his father long after he'd finished speaking.

"Hold it, youngbloods. Hold on a damn minute. I gotta catch me some sleep and get to work in a coupla hours. Yawl bout to wear my ass out."

"Daddy."

"Oh damn, I'm sorry. Sorry." The brother made two huge X's in the air and dropped his head shamefaced till his daughter laughed.

"Man, you got kids?"

"Yeah" was all Cliff said, not sure what else he could offer. It had been pleasant up to then, the brother easy to be easy with. But now he seemed to be waiting for Cliff to share what Cliff wasn't sure he had to share. He bent to take a drink. "Daughter," he offered, trying to calculate her age. He'd always used the Bay of Pigs invasion as a guide.

"They sompthin, ain't they?" the brother broke in, his children dragging him off to the door. "Take it slow, my man."

Cliff nodded and bent for another drink. Bay of Pigs was the spring of '61. His daughter had been born that summer. He bit his lip. Hell, how many fathers could just tick off the ages of their children, right off the bat? Not many. But then if the brother had put the question to him, as Aisha had the day before—What sort of person is your daughter?—Cliff would not have known how to answer. He let the water bubble up against closed lips for a while, not sure what that fact said about the man he was, or at least had thought he was, hoped he was, had planned to be for so long, was convinced when still a boy he could be once he got out of that house of worrisome women.

Aisha had come quietly up behind him and linked arms. "Hey, mister," she cooed, "how bout taking a po' colored gal to dinner." She pulled him away from the water fountain. "I'm starving."

Starving. Cliff looked at her quickly, but she did not react. Starving. He stared at her, but she was checking the buttons on her blouse, then stepping back for him to catch the door. She moved out swiftly and down the stairs ahead of him, not so much eager to get away, for she'd said how much she liked her job at the clinic. But eager to be done with it for the day and be with him. She waited at the foot of the stairs and linked arms again.

Cliff smiled. He dug her. Had known her less than a week, but felt he knew her. A chick who dealt straight up. No funny changes to go through. He liked the way she made it clear that she dug him.

"Whatcha grinnin about?" she asked, adjusting her pace to his. She was a brisk walker—he had remarked on it the day before—Northern urban brisk. I bet you like to lead too when you dance, he had teased her.

"Thinking about the first time I called you," he said.

"Oh? Oh." She nodded and was done, as though in that split second she had retrieved the tape from storage, played it, analyzed his version of what went down, and knew exactly what he had grinned about and that was that. He had kidded her about that habit too. "You mean the way I push for clarity, honesty?"

That was what he had meant, but he didn't like the cocky way she said it with the phony question mark on the end. She was a chick who'd been told she was too hard, too sure, too swift, and had made adjustments here and there, softening the edges. He wasn't sure that was honest of her, though he'd never liked women with hard edges.

"No," he half-lied. "Your sensitivity. I like the way you said, after turning me down for a drink, 'Hey, Brother—' "

"I called you Cliff. I'm not interested in being your sister."

He hugged her arm. "Okay, 'Hey, Cliff,' you said, 'I ain't rejecting you, but I don't drink, plus I got to get up at the crack of dawn tomorrow to prepare for a workshop. How about dinner instead?' "

"And that tickles you?"

"It refreshes me," he said, laughing, feeling good. It wasn't so easy being a dude, always putting yourself out there to be rejected. He'd never much cared for aggressive women; on the other hand, he appreciated those who met him halfway. He slowed her down some more. "Hey, city girl," he drawled. "This here a country boy you walkin wid, ain't used to shoes yet. The restaurant'll be there. Don't close till late."

"I'm starving, fool. Come on and feed me. You can take off them shoes. I'll carry em."

He hugged her arm again and picked up his pace. It was silly, he told himself, these endless control games he liked to play with assertive types. He was feeling too good. But then he wasn't. Starving. She had raised that question: Can you swear no child of yours is starving to death? Not confronting him or even asking him, softening the edges, but addressing the workshop, reading off a list of questions that might get the discussion started. The brother next to him had slapped his knees with his cap and muttered, "Here we go again with some women lib shit." But a sister across the aisle had been more vocal, jumping up to say, "Run it down to the brothers. Let's just put them other questions on hold and stay with this one a while," she demanded. "Yeah, can you swear?" Her hot eyes sweeping the room. "Can you deal with that, you men in here? Can you deal with that one?"

The discussion got sidetracked, it'd seemed to Cliff at the time. Everybody talking at once, all up in each other's face. Paternity, birth control, genocide, responsibility, fathering, mothering, children, child support, warrants, the courts, prison. One brother had maintained with much heat that half the bloods behind the walls were put there by some vengeful bitch. Warriors for the revolution wasting away in the joint for nonsupport or some other domestic bullshit. "Well, that should point something out!" a sister in the rear had yelled, trying to be heard over a bunch of brothers who stood up to say big-mouth sisters like herself were responsible for Black misery.

Starving. Cliff had spaced on much of the discussion, thinking about his daughter Rhea. Going over in his mind what he might have said had he been there to hear Donna murmur, "Hey, Cliff, I think I missed my period." But he had been in the army. And later when the pregnancy was a certainty, he was in Norfolk, Virginia, on his way overseas, he thought. And all the way out of port he lay in his bunk, Donna's letter under his head, crinkly in the pillowcase, gassing with Carl Davis about that ever-breathtaking announcement that could wreck a perfectly fine relationship—Hey, baby, I think I'm pregnant.

He had not quite kept track of the workshop debate the night before, for he was thinking about parenthood, thinking too of his own parents, his mother ever on the move to someplace else his father'd been rumored to be but never was, dragging him and his little sister Alma all over the South till the relatives in Charlotte said whoa, sister, park em here. And he had grown up in a household of women only, women always. Crowded, fussed over, intruded upon, continually compared to and warned not to turn out like the dirty dog who'd abandoned Aunt Mavis or that no-good nigger who'd done Cousin Dorcas dirty or some other low-down bastard that didn't mean no woman no good.

"You're unusually preoccupied, Cliff," Aisha was saying gently, as if reluctant to intrude, but hesitant about leaving him alone to wrassle with the pain he was sure was readable in his face. "Not that I know you well enough to know what's usual." He followed her gaze toward the park. "You feel like walking a while? Talking? Or maybe just being quiet?"

"Thought you were starving?" He heard an edge to his voice, but she didn't seem to notice.

"I am. I am." She waited at the curb, ready to cross over to the park or straight ahead to the Indian restaurant. Cliff disengaged his arm and fished out a cigarette, letting the light change. Had he been alone, he would have crossed over to the park. He had put off taking inventory for too long, his life was in a drift, unmonitored. Just that morning shaving, trying to fix in his mind what role he'd been called on to play in the impending student takeover, he'd scanned the calendar over the sink. The student demands would hit the campus paper on the anniversary of the Bay of Pigs.

He'd made certain promises that day, that spring day in '61 when the boat shipped out for Vietnam they'd thought, but headed directly for the Caribbean. He'd made certain promises about what his life would be like in five years, ten years, ever after if he lived. Had made certain promises to himself, to the unborn child, to God, he couldn't remember to whom, as the ship of Puerto Ricans, Chicanos and Bloods were cold-blood-edly transported without their knowing from Norfolk to Cuba to kill for all the wrong reasons. Then the knowledge of where they were and what they were expected to do, reminded of the penalty for disobeying orders, he'd made promises through clenched teeth, not that he was any clearer about the Cuban Revolution than he was about the Vietnamese struggle, but he knew enough about Afro-Cuban music to make some connec-tions and conclude that the secret mission was low-down. Knew too that if they died, no one at home'd be told the truth. Missing in action overseas. Taken by the Vietcong. Killed in Nam in the service of God and country.

"Worries?" Aisha asked, "or just reminiscing?"

He put his arm around her shoulders and hugged her close. His life was not at all the way he'd promised. "I was just thinking," he said slowly, crossing them toward the restaurant, "about the first time I came North as a kid." He wasn't sure that was a lie. The early days came crowding in on him every time he thought of his daughter and the future. And his daugh-ter filled his mind on every mention of starving.

He hadn't even known as a boy that he was or for what, till that Sunday his aunts had hustled him and Alma to the train depot. But Granddaddy Mobley didn't even get off the train when it slowed. Just leaned down and hauled them up by the wrists, first Alma, then him.

"Hop aboard, son," he'd said, bouncing the cigar to the back of his jaw. "This what you call a rescue job."

Son. He had been sugar dumpling, sweetie pie, honey dar-ling for so long, as though the horror of Southern living in general, the bitterness of being in particular some poor father-less child could be sweetened with a sugar tit, and if large enough could fill him up, fill up those drafty places somewhere inside. So long hugged and honey-bunched, he didn't know he was starving or for what till "son" was offered him and the grip on his wrist became a handshake man to man.

Dumfounded, the women were trotting along after the still-moving train, Cousin Dorcas calling his name, Aunt Evelyn calling Granddaddy Mobley a bunch of names.

"Train, iz you crazy?!" Aunt Mavis had demanded when she realized that was all the train intended to do, slow up for hopping off or kidnapping. "Have you lost your mind?" Cliff could never figure to whom this last remark was said. But he remembered he laughed like hell.

Granddaddy Mobley chuckled too, watching Cousin Dorcas through the gritty windows, trotting along the landing, shaking her fist, dodging the puffs of steam and the chunks of gravel thrown up by the wheels, the ribbons of her hat flying in and out of her shouting mouth.

Leaning out of an open window over his sister's head, Cliff could make out the women on the landing getting smaller, staring pop-eyed and pop-mouthed too. And when he glanced down, li'l Alma was looking straight up into his face the way she did from the bunk beds when the sun came up, the look asking was was everything okay and could the day begin. He grinned back out the window, and grinned too at his sister cause yeah, everything would be all right. He couldn't blame the women, though, for carrying on like that, having taken all morning to get the chicken fried and the rugs swept and the sheets boiled and dough beat up. Then come to find ole Mobley, highstepping, fun-loving, outrageous, drinking, rambler, gambler and everything else necessary to thoroughly scandalize the family name, upset the household with his annual visits, giving them something to talk about as the lamps glowed at night till next visiting time, ole Mobley wasn't even thinking about a visit at all this time. Wasn't even stopping long enough to say hello tc his daughter, not that she was there. Just came to snatch the darling little girl and the once perfect little gentleman now grown rusty and hardheaded just like his daddy for the world.

"We going North with you?" Alma had asked, not believing she could go anywhere without her flouncy dresses, her ribbons, and their mother's silver hairbrush from the world's fair.

"That's right."

"We going to live with you?" young Cliff had pressed, eager to get things straight. "To live with you till we grown or just for summer or what?"

Instead of answering, the old man whipped out a wad of large, white handkerchiefs and began to unfold them with very large gestures. The children settled in their seats waiting for the magic show to commence. But the old man just spread them out on the seats, three for sitting on and one for his hat. Cliff and Alma exchanged a look, lost for words. And in that moment, the old man leaned forward, snatched Alma's little yellow-haired doll and pitched it out the window.

"And you better not cry," he said.

"No, ma'am."

Cliff laughed and the old man frowned. "Unless you in training to take care of white folks' babies when you grown."

"No, ma'am."

Cliff had smiled smugly, certain that Alma had no idea what this rescue man was saying. He did. And he looked forward to growing up with a man like this. Alma slid her small hand into his and Cliff squeezed it. And not once did she look back after her doll, or he at the town.

"I met your wife in the bus terminal—"

"Ex-wife," Cliff said, jolted out of his reverie.

136

Aisha poured the tea. "Ex-wife. Met her last Monday and—"

"You told me."

"I didn't tell you the whole thing."

Cliff looked up from his plate of meat patties. He wasn't sure he wanted to hear about it. Every time he had tried to think of his daughter, he discovered he couldn't detach her from the woman he'd married. Thinking about Donna made him mad. Thinking about his daughter Rhea just made him breathless. Rising, he jingled change in his pocket and stalled for time at the jukebox. That was the first thing Aisha had said to him when they were introduced just four days ago on campus. "Hemphill? I think I know your wife, Donna Hemphill. Ran into her at the bus terminal less than an hour ago."

After his one class of the day and a quick meeting with the Black student union, he'd sought her out in the faculty dining room, convinced his chairman would at least give her the semi-deluxe treatment, particularly considering his taste for black meat (or so the rumor went, though he rarely did more toward orienting new faculty members than pointing out their cubicle, shoving a faculty handbook at them, and warning them about the "Mau Mau," his not-so-affectionate name for the Black student union). She had pursued the topic the minute Cliff had seated himself next to her, remarking quietly that his wife had seemed on the verge of collapse. He welcomed the mention of Donna only for the opportunity it offered to point out that one, she was very much an ex, two he was single, three he found her, Aisha, attractive. Beyond that, he could care less about Donna or her mental state. Aisha had remarked then— too sarcastically for his taste—that this very ex-wife with the mental state was the woman who was raising his daughter. He had eaten the dry roast beef sullenly, grateful for the appearance of his colleague Robinson, who swung the conversation toward the students and the massive coronaries they were causing in administrative circles.

Some Indian movie music blared out at Cliff's back as he picked out one of the umpteen rhythms to stroll back to the table doing, slapping out the beat on his thigh.

"I didn't say this before"—Aisha was reaching for the drumming hand—"cause you cut me short last Tuesday. I'm sorry I didn't press it then on campus, cause it's harder now . . . that I know you . . . and all."

"Then forget it."

She slid her hand back to her side of the table and busied herself with the meat patties. He drummed on the table with both hands, trying to read her mood. He felt he owed her some explanation, wanted even to talk this thing out, his feelings about his daughter. Then resented Aisha for that. He drummed away. The last thing he would have wanted for this evening, the first time they'd been together with no other appointments to cut into their time, the last thing he wanted, feeling already a little off-center, crowded, was a return to that part of his history that seemed so other, over with, some dim drama starring a Cliff long since discarded. Cliff the soldier, Cliff the young father, Cliff the sociology instructor—there was clarity if not continuity. But Cliff the husband . . . blank.

He had pronounced the marriage null and void in the spring of '61. On the troop ship speeding to who knew where, or at least none of the dudes in that battalion knew yet, but to die most probably. He'd read the letter over and over, and was convinced Donna was lying about being pregnant and so far advanced. He was due home for good soon, and this was her way to have him postpone thinking of a split. He and Carl

Davis had gassed the whole time out of port about what they were going to do with their lives if they still had them in five months' time. Then some of the soldiers were saying the fleet was in the Caribbean. And all hell broke loose, the men mistakenly assuming—assuming, then readying up for shore leave in Trinidad. The CO told them different, though not much. First there was a sheaf of papers that had to be signed, or court-martial, papers saying they never would divulge to press, to family, to friends, even to each other anything at all regarding the secret mission they were about to embark upon. Then they got their duties. Most work detail the same—painting over the ship's numbers, masking all U.S. identification, readying up the equipment for the gunners, checking their packs and getting new issues of ammunition.

"We're headed for Cuba," Carl Davis had said.

"That's crazy. The action's in Vietnam."

"Mate, I'm telling you, we're off to Cuba. T.J. was upside and got the word. The first invasionary battalions are Cuban exiles. They'll hook up with the forces there on the island to overthrow Fidel Castro."

"You got to be kidding."

Carl had sneered at Cliff's naïveté. "Mate, they got air coverage that'd made the Luftwaffe look silly. We rendezvous with a carrier and a whole fleet of marines moving in from Nicaragua. I'm telling you, this is it."

T.J. had skidded down the stair rail and whispered. "They got Kennedy on a direct line. Kennedy! Jim, this operation is being directed from the top."

"Holy shit." Cliff had collapsed on his bunk, back pack and all, the letter crumpling under his ear. A child was being born soon, the letter said. He was going to be a father. And if he died, what would happen to his child? His marriage had been in shreds before he'd left, a mere patchwork job on the last leave, and she'd been talking of going back home. His child. Her parents. That world. Those people.

"I never knew Donna well," Aisha was saying. "We worked at Family Services and I used to see her around, jazz concerts, the clubs. I pretty much wrote her off as a type. One of those gray girls who liked to follow behind Black musicians, hang out and act funky."

Cliff looked at Aisha quickly. Was she the type to go for blood? He'd had enough of the white girl–brother thing. Had been sick of it all, of hearing, of reading about it, of arguing, of defending himself, even back then on the tail end of the Bohemian era, much less in the Black and Proud times since.

"Use to run into her a lot when I lived downtown. The baby didn't surprise me—hell, half of Chelsea traffic was white girls pushing mulatto babies in strollers. We used to chat. You two seemed to be always on the verge of breakup, and she was forever going down in flames. I got the impression the baby was something of . . . a hostage?" She seemed to wait for his response. He blanked his face out. "A hostage," she continued, seeming to relish the word, "as per usual."

The waiter slid a dish of chutney at Cliff's elbow, then leaned in to replace the teapot with a larger, steamier one. Cliff leaned back as the plates and bowls were taken from the tray in some definite, mysterious order and placed just so on the table. Cliff rearranged the plate of roti and the cabbage. The waiter looked at him and placed them in their original spots. Cliff sneaked a look at Aisha and they shared a stone-faced grin.

"Cliff?" She seemed to call to him, the him behind his poker face. He leaned forward. Whatever she had to say, it'd be over with soon and they could get on with the Friday evening he had in mind.

"I asked Donna on Tuesday to give up the child. To give

your daughter to me. I'm prepared to raise—"

Cliff stared, not sure he heard that right.

"Look. She's standing in the bus terminal having a crying jag, listing fifty-leven different brands of humiliations and bump-offs from the Black community. She's been trying to enroll your daughter in an independent Black school, at a Yoruba cultural center, at the Bedford-Stuyvesant—"

"Bedford-Stuyvesant?"

"Yeah, your wife lives in Brooklyn."

"Ex-wife."

Aisha spread her napkin and asked very pointedly, "You were not aware that your daughter's been living in Brooklyn for two years?" Cliff tried to remember the last address he had sent money to, recalled he had always given it to Alma. But then Alma had moved to the coast last spring . . .

"Hey, look, Cliff, I've noticed the way you keep leaning on this 'ex' business. I'm sure you're sick to death of people jumping on you, especially sisters, about the white-woman thing. Quite frankly I don't give a shit who you married or who you are . . . not now . . . I only thought I did," she said, spacing her words out in a deliberate challenge. "What does interest me is the kid. I'll tell you just what I told her, I'm prepared to take the girl—"

"Hold it. Hold it." Cliff shoved his plate away and tried to sort out what he was hearing. If only he could have a tape of this, he was thinking, to play at his leisure, not have to respond or be read. "Back up, you're moving too fast for me. I'm just a country boy." He smiled, not surprised that she did smile back. She looked tired.

"Okay. She's been trying to move your daughter into cultural activities and whatnot. Very concerned about the kid's racial identity. For years she's always been asking me to suggest places to take her and how to handle things and so forth. So

I'm standing in the bus terminal while this white woman falls apart on me, asking to be forgiven her incompetence, her racism, her hysteria. And I'm pissed. So I ask her—"

"Where's the nigger daddy who should be taking the weight."

Aisha studied her fork and resumed eating. Cliff clenched his jaws. She was eating now as though she'd been concentrating on that chicken curry for hours, had not even spoken, did not even know he was there. Was that the point of it all, to trigger that outburst? And it had been an outburst, his face was still burning. Was she out for blood? It was a drag. Cliff reached for the chutney and sensed her tense up. She looked coiled on her side of the table, mouth full of poisonous fangs. She was a type, he decided, a type he didn't like. She had seemed a groovy woman, but she was just another bitch. She had looked good to him less than half an hour ago, bouncing around in the white space shoes. Had looked good in that slippery white uniform wrinkling at her hips. And all he thought he wanted to do was take her to his place and tell her so, show her. He thought he still might like to take her home to make love to her—no, to fuck her. The atmosphere kept changing, the tone, the whole quality of his feelings for her kept shifting. She kept him off balance. Yeh, he'd like to fuck her, but not cause she looked good. Cliff tore off a piece of roti, then decided he didn't want it. Looked at her and decided he was being absurd. What had she said she was pissed about? Donna, an unhinged white woman raising a Black child. Why had he been so defensive?

"This was a bad time to meet," he heard himself saying. "I wish we had met at some other time when—"

"Look, sugar," she spat out with a malice that didn't match the words, "no matter when or where or how we met, the father question would've come up. And I'd have had to judge

142

what kind of man you are behind your whole sense of what it means to bring a child into the world. I'm funny that way, mister."

"What I was thinking was," he pressed on, shoving aside the anger brewing, clamping down hard on the urge to bust her in the jaw, not sure the urge to hold her close wasn't just as strong, "in a year or so you might have met me with my daughter. I've been considering for a long time fighting for custody of Rhea."

"How long?"

"Off and on for years. But here lately, last few weeks . . ." It occurred to him that that was exactly what he'd been trying to pull together in his mind, a plan. That was what had been crowding him.

"Donna said she'd talk to you about it, Cliff, then get back to me. It was a serious proposal I was making."

"She hasn't called me. Matter of fact, we haven't talked in years."

"Uh-hunh." She delivered this with the jauntiness of a gum-cracking sister from Lenox Avenue. Cliff read on her face total disbelief of all he'd said, as though he couldn't have been really considering it and not talk with the child's mother. He was pissed off. How did it get to be her business, any of it?

"Anyway, Brother," she said, shifting into still another tone, "I'm prepared to take the child. I've got this job at the clinic, it'll hold me till summer when the teaching thing comes through. My aunt runs a school up on Edgecombe. She's not the most progressive sister in the world, but the curriculum's strong academically. And there're several couples on my block who get together and take the kids around. I'm good with children. Raised my nephews and my sisters. I'd do right by the little girl, Cliff. What do you want to ask me?"

Her voice had faded away to a whisper. She sipped her tea now, and for a minute he thought she was about to cry. He wasn't sure for what, but felt he was being unjustly blamed for something. She hadn't believed him. That made him feel unsure about himself. He watched her, drifting in and out among the fragments of sensations, questions that wouldn't stay formed long enough for him to get a hold of. He studied her until his food got cold.

She wasn't going to sleep with him, that was clear. He knew from past experiences that the moment had passed, that moment when women resolved the tension by deciding yes they would, then relaxed one way, or no they wouldn't, and eased into another rhythm. Often at the critical point, especially with younger women, he'd step into their timing and with one remark or a caress of the neck could turn the moment in his favor. He hadn't even considered it with Aisha. There had seemed time enough to move leisurely, no rush. They'd had dinner that first night, then he'd had a Black faculty meeting. He'd picked her up last night to get to the workshop, and after they'd had coffee with Acoli and Essa and talked way into the night about the students' demands. He hadn't even considered that this evening, which just a half-hour ago seemed stretched out so casual and unrushed, would turn out as anything but right.

Hell, they weren't children. They had established right from the jump that this would be a relationship, a relationship of meaning. And he'd looked forward to it, had even thought of calling Alma long distance and working Aisha somehow into the conversation. He knew it would please his sister, for he knew well how it pained her whenever he launched into his dissertation on Black women, the bitterness for those Black women who had raised him surfacing always, and for the others so much like them—though Alma argued it wasn't so—who'd stepped into his life with such explosions, leaving ashes in their wake. And Alma argued that wasn't so either, just his own blindness contracted from poisons he should have pumped out somehow long ago cause they weren't reasonably come by either. He was sick of his dissertation, the arguing, the venom, even thinking about it.

"You can imagine, Cliff . . . well, the irony of it all, meeting you right after seeing Donna after all these years of running into her, hearing about you . . . Look, it's very complicated—my feelings about . . . the whole thing."

"How so?" He poured the last of the hot tea into her cup and waited. She seemed to study the cup for a long time as though considering whether to reject it, wait for it to cool, drink it, or maybe fling it in his face. He couldn't imagine why that last seemed such a possibility. His sister Alma would have argued that he simply expected the worst always and usually got it, provoked it.

"On the one hand, I'm very attracted to you, Cliff. You care about the students. I mean . . . well, you have a reputation on campus for being—" She was blushing and that surprised the hell out of him. He decided he didn't know women at all. They were too weird, all of them. "Well, for being one of the good guys. Plus you so sharp, ya know, and a great sense of humor. Not to mention you fine." She was looking suddenly girlish. He wanted to laugh, but he didn't want to interrupt her. He was liking this. "And I dig being with you. You're comfortable, even when you're drifting off, you're comfortable to be with." He bowed in his seat. They were smiling again.

"On the other hand"—she cocked her head to signal she hoped to get through this part with the same chumminess—"well . . ." She drank the tea now, two fingers pressed on each side of the Oriental cup, her face moving into the steam, lips pursing to blow. If they ever got around to the pillow talk, he'd ask her about her gesture and whether or not it had been designed to get him. He found all this blowing and sipping very arousing, for no reason he could think of.

"On the other hand," she said again, "while you seem to be a principled person . . . I mean, clearly you're not a bastard or a coward . . . not handling the shit on campus like you been doing . . . but—" She put the cup down.

"Hey look. It's like this, Cliff. I don't understand brothers who marry white girls, I really don't. And I really don't see how you can just walk away from the kid, let your child just . . . Well, damn, what is your daughter, a souvenir?" It was clear to Cliff that his reaction was undisguised and that she was having no trouble reading his face. "Perhaps"—she was looking hopeful now, his cue to rise to the occasion—"perhaps you really have been trying to figure out how to do it, how to get custody?"

"I considered it long before we even broke up. When I first heard that the child was an actual fact, was about to be born, I was in the army. As a matter of fact, I was up to my neck in the Bay of Pigs shit." He had never discussed it before, was amazed he could do it now, could relate it all in five or six quick sentences, when times earlier he hadn't even been able to pull it together coherently in a whole night, staring at the ceiling, wondering how many brothers had been rerouted to the Philippines to put down the resistance to Marcos and the corporate bosses, how many to Ethiopia to vamp on the Eritrean Front, and how many would wind up in southern Africa all too soon, thinking they were going who knew where. How many more caught in the trick bag of colored on colored death if all who knew remained silent on the score, chumps afraid of change?

Cliff had always maintained he despised people who saw and heard but would not move on what they knew. His colleagues who could wax lyric analyzing the hidden agenda of SEEK and other OEO circuses engineered to fail, but did nothing about it. Bloods in his department grooming the students for caretaker positions, all the while screaming on the system, the oppression, hawking revolution, but carefully cultivating caretakers to negotiate a separate peace for a separate piece of the corrupt pie, claiming the next generation would surely do it. And even Cousin Dorcas and Aunt Mavis years before, going through a pan of biscuits and a pot of coffee laying out with crystal clarity the madness of his mother's life, chronically on hold till she could just get to that one more place to find the man never where folks said he'd be. But never once wrassling the woman, their sister, their kin, to the floor, demanding she at least put the children on her agenda, if not herself. And Cliff himself, heroic in spots, impotent in others, he had postponed for too long an inventory of his self, his life.

"The Cuban people were ready. They kicked our ass. That first landing troop ran smack into an alligator farm in Playa Girón and got wiped out. The second got wasted fore they even got off the beach. And all the while our ship was getting hit. Cannonballs sailing right between the smoke stacks of the ship. And Kennedy on the line saying, 'Pull back,' realizing them balls were a warning, a reminder of what could happen in the world if the U.S. persisted."

Aisha poured him a glass of ginger beer and waited for him to continue. Cliff felt opened up like he hadn't been in years.

"The idea that I might be killed, that my wife Donna would move back to her parents, my child growing up in an all-white environment . . . I use to run the my-wife-is-an-individual-white-person number . . . I dunno . . . it all scared the shit out of me," he was saying, not able to find the bridge, the connection, the transition from those thoughts, those promises made in Cuban waters and what in fact he lived out later and called his life.

"When we broke up, I turned my back, I guess," he said, finding his place again, but not the bridge. "I use to see my

147

daughter a lot when my sister Alma lived in the city. And if I could just figure out how to manage it all, have time for my work and—"

"Your work?" she said, clutching the tablecloth. "Your work?" she sneered. "You one of those dudes who thinks his 'real' work is always outside of—separate from—oh, shit."

He felt her withdraw. He would make an effort to draw her out again, even if she came out blazing in a hot tirade about "women's work" and "men's work" and "what a load of horseshit." He would do it for himself. Later for the them that might have been.

"We were discussing all this recently in class—'The Black Family in the Twentieth Century,' my new course."

"Yeah, I know," she said.

"You know?"

"My niece is in your class. She tapes your lectures. Big fan of yours, my niece."

"Oh." Cliff couldn't remember now just what he had wanted to say, had lost the thread. Aisha had motioned the waiter over and was scanning the dessert list. He shook his head. Dessert was not what he wanted at this point.

He had handed back the students' research papers on their own families when the vet who sat in the back got up to say how odd it was that their generation, meaning the sophomores or juniors, despite the persistent tradition in their own families of folks raising children not their own, odd that this younger generation felt exempt. How many here, someone in the front of the room had asked then, can see themselves adopting children or taking in a kid from the streets, or from a strung-out neighbor, as their own? Cliff had expected a split down the middle, the brothers opting for pure lineage, the sisters charging ego and making a case for "the children" rather than "my child." But it didn't go down that way. The discussion never got off the ground. And after class, the vet had criticized Cliff for short-circuiting the discussion. Cliff hadn't seen his point then. But now, watching Aisha coax the recipe for some dessert or other from the waiter, he could admit that he had probably spaced.

Naturally he'd been thinking of his daughter Rhea, wondering how many others in the class had children and whether it would be fruitful to ask that first. The problem was, he could never think of Rhea without also thinking of Donna. Even after he refused to visit the child on his wife's turf, preferring the serenity of Alma's home for the visits, Rhea was still daughter to the woman who'd been his wife. And he was outside.

He'd been so proud when as a baby she had learned to say "Daddy" first. That had knocked him out. His sister had offered some psycholinguistic-somethinorother explanation, completely unsolicited and halfway unheard, about a baby's physical capacity to produce d sounds long before m sounds. Cliff paid Alma no mind.

But as the baby grew more independent, more exploratory of the world beyond her skin, he realized why she could say "Daddy" so much sooner. Cause Mommy was not separate, Mommy was part of the baby's world, attached to her own ego. He was distinctly different. Outside. It was some time before Mommy was seen as other. And still later that Rhea could step back from herself and manage "Rhea," then "me." Meanwhile he was outside. Way before that even he was outside—pregnancy, labor, delivery, breastfeeding. Women and babies, mothers and children, mother and child. Him outside. If only she had looked more like him, though in fact she resembled Alma more than Donna. But still there was distance. He knew no terms for negotiating a relationship with her that did not also include her mother. How had Donna managed that? Hostage, Aisha had said.

He chuckled to himself and stared at Aisha. He started up a nutty film in his head. All over the country, sisters crouching behind bushes with croaker sacks ready to pounce and spirit away little mulatto babies. Mulatto babies were dearer, prizer. Or sisters shouting from the podiums, the rooftops, the bedrooms, telling warriors dirty diapers was revolutionary work. Sisters coiled in red leather booths mesmerizing fathers into a package deal. He clamped down hard on fantasies leaching poisons into his brain. Package deal—me and the kid.

"Were you proposing to me by any chance?" he asked just for the hell of it.

"Say what?" She first looked bewildered, then angry, then amazed. She burst out laughing, catching him off-guard when she asked in icy tones, "Is that basically your attitude? Big joke?"

He shrugged in innocence and decided to leave it alone. She was bristly. Let her eat her pastry and drink her mint tea, he instructed himself. Put her in a cab and send her home. He wanted time to himself, time to take a good look at the yellow chair Alma had bequeathed to him when she moved to the coast. Its unfolding capacity never failed to amaze him. It would make a better bed than the Disney pen he'd spied in a children's store that morning. He was feeling good again.

He leaned forward and Aisha slid a forkful of crumbly pastry into his mouth. She was looking good to him once more. He grinned. She jerked her chin as if to ask what was he about to say. He wasn't about to say anything. But he was thinking that no, they hadn't met at the wrong time. It'd been the right time for him. The wrong time for them maybe. But what the hell.

"What did you want to be when you grew up?" she asked.

A Tender Man

He leaned in for another forkful of pastry. "Just don't be like your daddy" rang in his ears. "A tender man," he said and watched her lashes flutter lower.

The question he would put to himself when he got home and stretched out in that yellow chair was what had he promised his daughter in the spring of '61. He smiled at Aisha and leaned up out of his chair to kiss her on the forehead. She blushed. He was sure he could come true for the Cliff he'd been.

A
Girl's
Story

She was afraid to look at herself just yet. By the time I count to twenty, she decided, if the bleeding hasn't stopped . . . she went blank. She hoisted her hips higher toward the wall. Already her footprints were visible. Sweat prints on the wall, though she was shivering. She swung her feet away from the map she'd made with Dada Bibi, the map of Africa done in clay and acrylics. The bright colors of Mozambique distracted her for a moment. She pictured herself in one of the wraps Dada Bibi had made for them to dance in. Pictured herself in Africa talking another language in that warm, rich way Dada Bibi and the brother who tutored the little kids did. Peaceful, friendly, sharing.

Rae Ann swept through her head again for other possible remedies to her situation. For a nosebleed, you put your head way back and stuffed tissue up your nostrils. Once she'd seen her brother Horace plaster his whole set of keys on the back of the neck. The time he had the fight with Joe Lee and his nose bled. Well, she'd tried ice cubes on the neck, on the stomach, on the thighs. Had stuffed herself with tissue. Had put her hips atop a pile of sofa cushions. And still she was bleeding. And what was she going to do about M'Dear's towels? No one would miss the panties and skirt she'd bundled up in the bottom of the garbage. But she couldn't just disappear a towel, certainly not two. M'Dear always counted up the stacks of laundry before the Saturday put-away.

Rae Ann thought about Dada Bibi over at the Center. If the shiny-faced woman were here now with her, it wouldn't be so bad. She'd know exactly what to do. She would sit in the chair and examine Rae Ann's schoolbooks. Would talk calmly. Would help her. Would tell her there was nothing to worry about, that she was a good girl and was not being punished. Would give an explanation and make things right. But between the house and the Center she could bleed to death.

Between her bed and the toilet she'd already left many a trail. Had already ragged the green sponge a piece, scrubbing up after herself. If Horace came home, she could maybe ask him to run over to the Center. Cept he'd want to know what for. Besides, he didn't go round the Center any more since they jumped on his case so bad about joining the army. He didn't want to hear no more shit about the Vietnamese were his brothers and sisters, were fighting the same enemy as Black folks and was he crazy, stupid or what. And he surely wouldn't want to have to walk all the long way back alone with Dada Bibi in her long skirt and turban, trying to make conversation and getting all tongue-tied sliding around the cussin he always did, and everybody checking them out walking as they were toward his house and all. But maybe if she told him it was an emergency and cried hard, he wouldn't ask her nothing, would just go.

Yesterday Dada Bibi had hugged her hello and didn't even

fuss where you been little sister and why ain't you been coming round, don't you want to know about your heritage, ain't you got no pride? Dada Bibi never said none of them things ever. She just hugged you and helped you do whatever it was you thought you came to do at the Center. Rae Ann had come to cut a dress for graduation. She'd be going to intermediate in the fall, and that was a big thing. And maybe she had come to hear about the African queens. Yesterday as they sewed, Dada Bibi told them about some African queen in the old days who kept putting off marriage cause she had to be a soldier and get the Europeans out the land and stop the slaving.

She liked the part where Dada Bibi would have the dude come over to propose umpteen times. Rae Ann could just see him knocking real polite on the screen door and everything. Not like Horace do, or like Pee Wee neither, the boy she was halfway liking but really couldn't say she respected any. They just stood on the corner and hollered for their women, who had better show up quick or later for their ass.

Dada Bibi would have the dude say, "Well, darling, another harvest has past and I now have twenty acres to work and have started building on the new house and the cattle have multiplied. When can we marry?" And then Dada Bibi would have the sister say, "My husband-to-be, there are enemies in the land, crushing our people, our traditions underfoot. We must raise an army and throw them out." And then the dude would go sell a cow or something and help organize the folks on the block to get guns and all. And the sister would get the black-smith to make her this bad armor stuff. Course Gretchen got to interrupt the story to say the sister chumping the dude, taking his money to have her some boss jewelry made and what a fool he was. But the girls tell her to hush so they can hear the rest. Dada Bibi maintaining it's important to deal with how

Gretchen seeing things go down. But no one really wants to give Gretchen's view a play.

Anyway, after many knocks on the screen door and raising of armies and battles, the two of them are old-timers. Then the sister finally says, "My husband-to-be, there is peace in the land now. The children are learning, the folks are working, the elders are happy, our people prosper. Let us get married on the new moon." Gretchen got to spoil it all saying what old folks like that need to get married for, too old to get down anyway. And Dada Bibi try to get the girls to talk that over. But they just tell Gretchen to shut her big mouth and stop hogging all the straight pins. Rae Ann liked to retell the stories to the kids on the block. She always included Gretchen's remarks and everybody's response, since they seemed, in her mind, so much a part of the story.

Rae Ann's legs were tiring. Her left foot was stinging, going to sleep. Her back hurt. And her throat was sore with tension. She looked up at the map and wondered if Dada Bibi had seen the whole trouble coming. When Rae Ann had stayed behind to clean up the sewing scraps, the woman had asked her if there was anything she wanted to talk about now she was getting to be such a young woman. And Rae Ann had hugged her arms across her chest and said, "No, ma'am," cause she figured she might have to hear one of them one-way talks like M'Dear do about not letting boys feel on your tits. But when she got ready to leave, Dada Bibi hugged her like she always did, even to the girls who squirmed out of her reach and would rather not even wave hello and goodbye, just come in and split at their leisure.

"My sister," she had said into her ear, gently releasing her with none of the embarrassed shove her relatives seemed to always punctuate their embraces with. "You're becoming a woman and that's no private thing. It concerns us all who love you. Let's talk sometimes?"

Rae Ann liked the way she always made it a question. Not like the teachers, who just flat-out told you you were going to talk, or rather they were going to talk at you. And not like M'Dear or Aunt Candy, who always just jumped right in talking without even a let's this or could we that.

Maybe Dada Bibi had seen something in her face, in her eyes. Or maybe there had been a telltale spot on the back of her jeans as early as yesterday. Rae Ann twisted her head around toward the pile of clothes on the back of her chair. Upside down her jeans were spotless. Well, then, she reasoned methodically, how did Dada Bibi know? But then who said she had known anything? "That ole plain-face bitch don't know nuthin" was Horace's word to the wise. But just the same, he hung around the bus stop on Tuesday nights, acting blasé like he didn't know Dada Bibi had Tuesday night classes at the college. Not that anybody would speak on this. Joe Lee had cracked and had his ass whipped for his trouble.

Rae Ann was smelling herself and not liking it. She'd already counted three sets of twenties, which meant it was time to move. She rejected the notion of a bath. The last bath had only made it worse. Fore she could even get one foot good out the water, red spots were sliding off the side of the tub onto the tile. She exhaled deeply and tried to make a list in her head. New tissue, tight pants to hold it all in place, the last of the ice tray still in the sink on her twat. She closed her eyes and moaned. Her list was all out of order. She tried again. Check floors and tub. Put towels in bottom of garbage. Put garbage out. Scrape carrots and make salad. Secrete a roll of tissue in her closet for later. Get to the Center. She opened her eyes. What would she say?

Rae Ann pulled her legs down and swung off the bed. She checked to see that the newspaper was still in place before drawing the covers up. She stood and parted the flaps of her bathrobe. Last time she had moved too quickly and the oozing had started, a blob of syrupy brown slipping down the inside of her leg and she afraid to touch it, to stop it, just stood there like a simpleton till it reached her ankle, and then she fled into the bathroom too late. She was looking into the toilet as the water swirled away the first wad of tissue. What if the toilet stuffed up, backed up on the next flush? She could imagine M'Dear bellowing the roof down as the river of red overran the rim and spilled over onto the tiles, flooding the bathroom, splashing past the threshold and onto the hall linoleum.

"Get out the bathroom, willya damn it!"

She jumped and banged an elbow on the sink. She hadn't heard Horace come into the house. He usually announced his arrivals by singing, stamping, and doing a bump-de-bump against the furniture. Had thought she was all alone with her terror. Hadn't even locked the door and here she was with her pants down and the last clump of tissue shredding, sticky red.

"Come on now. I gotta shower fore M'Dear get home."

She was trapped. If she unhooked the roll of toilet paper to take into her room, he'd see that. And M'Dear would be in any minute and would come into her room to set her bags down and get her slippers. If she hid in the closet and squatted down behind the bundles of mothballed blankets . . .

"Hey," Horace was bamming on the door. "You okay?"

Something in her brother's voice startled her. Before she could stop herself she was brimming over and shivering hard.

"Rae Ann?" he called through the door. "Rachel?"

"Don't come in!" she screamed. "Don't come in."

The doorknob was being held in position, she could see that.

It had stopped turning. And it seemed to her that he was holding his breath on his side of the door just like she was holding hers on hers.

"Hey," he whispered "you okay?" When she didn't answer, he let go of the knob. She watched it move back into place and then heard him walk away. She sat there hugging herself, trying to ease the chattering of her teeth. She leaned over to yank her washcloth off the hook. And then the smell gripped her. That smell was in everything. In her bed, her clothes, her breath. The smell of death. A dry, rank graveyard smell. The smell of her mother's sickroom years ago, so long ago all the memory that had survived was the smell and the off-yellow color from the lamp, a color she'd never ever seen again anywhere. A brown stain was smack in the middle of the washcloth. She flung it into the basin and ran the water.

"She in there crying."

Rae Ann's heart stopped. M'Dear was in the kitchen. Just behind the medicine cabinet, just behind the wall, they were talking about her. She jumped up and ran to the door.

"Don't be locking that door," the voice boomed through the wall. "We hear you in there."

"And we know what you been doin too," her brother's voice rang out. She wondered what happened to that something that was in his voice just minutes ago. Where had that brother gone to so quick? Maybe cause he was scared he sounded so nice. That time when Furman and his gang were after Pee Wee he had sounded like that. Up on the roof, scrunched between the pigeon coop and the chimney, Pee Wee revealed a voice Rae Ann had never known he had. Told her she was a nice girl and shouldn't mess around with guys like him, would have to be careful. Not at all the voice bragging on the handball court, Pee Wee mounting his motorbike, Pee Wee in the schoolyard smoking. Why did it take scarifying to bring out the voice?

"Horace just scared I may die in here and he won't be able to take his damn shower," she mumbled into the washcloth, gagging on the smell. She was too afraid to think anything else.

"You best get in here, Madame." The voice came at her through the mirror. Madame. She was freezing again. Madame never meant anything good. Madame, you best cut a switch. Madame, there's a letter here from school. Madame, where's the receipt from the telephone bill. Madame, do you think you too grown to mind.

Rae Ann swished around some mouthwash and rewrapped her bathrobe tight. She knew she was waddling, the minute she saw the way they looked at her, but she couldn't get herself together. Horace turned back to a plate in the icebox he was eating from. M'Dear was leaning up against the sink, her hat still on her head, the shopping bags leaning against her legs, her shoes not even unlaced.

"You had somebody in here?"

"No, ma'am."

"Ask her how come she in her bathrobe."

"You hush," the old woman warned, and Horace disappeared behind the icebox door.

"What you been doin?"

"Nothin."

"Don't tell me nothin when I'm trying to find out somethin. Miz Gladys run all the way up to the bus stop to tell me she seen you comin home from school way before three o'clock."

Rae Ann heard the pause, felt the pause on top of her head, weighing it down into her shoulders. She shrugged. She didn't know how to fill it and lift it.

"You play hookey from school today? Went somewhere with somebody?"

"No, ma'am."

M'Dear breathing in and out, the huffin-puffin getting

wheezy. It was clear Rae Ann had better say something, cause there wouldn't be too many more questions, just a heavier pausing swelling, swelling to crush her.

"You cold or somethin?" A question that came out finally and lifted her from her knees. She didn't know why she was so grateful to hear it. She hadn't expected it. Was nodding yes while her mouth said no and smiling and fixing to cry all at the same time.

"Tears don't tell me a damn thing, Rachel Ann."

"Tears say a whole lot to me," Horace was telling the toaster, singing it lest the woman get on him again for butting in.

"I sure wish you'd go somewhere," Rae Ann said over her shoulder. It might be easier to talk with just her grandmother. Though she was still a blank as to what she could possibly say to take the hardness out of her grandmother's face. M'Dear's eyes shot from the boy to the girl to the boy then back again, her head swiveling, her eyes flashing, like she was on the trail of something and there was danger sure for somebody.

"M'Dear, I'm bleeding," she heard herself say, huddling smaller into her bathrobe, feeling an oozing on the inside of her leg.

The old woman's face looked red-hot and strangled, and for a minute the girl thought she was going to be slapped.

"Whatcha been doin?" she hissed through clenched teeth. Rae Ann backed up as a whole bunch of questions and accusations tumbled out of the woman's mouth ramming into her. "You been to the barbershop, haven't you? Let that filthy man go up inside you with a clothes hanger. You going to be your mama all over again. Why didn't you come to me? Who's the boy? Tell me his name quick. And you better not lie."

M'Dear had snatched up her pocketbook, not waiting on an answer in the meantime, and was heading out the door, waving

Horace to come on. He burned his fingers pulling out the toast, eager for the adventure.

"I didn't do anything," Rae Ann screamed, racing to the door before it closed against the back of her brother. "I didn't do anything, I swear to God," her throat raspy, failing her, the words barely pushed out and audible.

"Oooooh," she heard echoing in the tiled hallway, the word hollow and cool, bouncing off the walls as the old woman shoved past the boy back into the kitchen. "Oh, my goodness," she said through her hands. And then Rae Ann felt the hands on her shoulders moist from the mouth coming right through the terry cloth. The hands giving slight pull, pat, tug but not a clear embrace. "Oh, Rachel Ann," the woman whispered, steering her gently down the hall. "Girl, why didn't you say so?" she said, helping her into bed.

Rae Ann bent her knees and eased herself down onto the newspapers. She watched the woman back out of the room, her hands smoothing her waistband, as though she were leaving the dishes to make a call or leaning up from the dough on the breadboard to shout across the air shaft to Miz Gladys. Smoothing the bulk that bunched up over the waistband, nervous.

"Be right back, sugar," still backing out the room. And Rae Ann glad she'd moved her sneakers out the doorway. That'd be all she needed, M'Dear falling over some sneakers.

"Hush your ugly mouth, cause you don't know what you talkin about," she heard in the kitchen just before the front door slammed. Was she going to get a doctor? Maybe she'd gone for Dada Bibi? That wasn't likely. I ain't studyin them folks over there, M'Dear and Miz Gladys like to say, sucking their teeth at the letters, flyers, posters, numerous papers that came into the block, the building, the house, explaining what the Center was about.

"I ain't nobody's African," Miz Gladys had said. "One hundred percent American and proud of it." And M'Dear had jerked her head in agreement, trashing the latest flyer Rae Ann had slipped onto the table.

Rae Ann had tried to push all they said up against other things in her head. Being American and being proud and they weren't the same in her head. When Dada Bibi talked about Harriet Tubman and them, she felt proud. She felt it in her neck and in her spine. When the brother who ran the program for the little kids talked about powerful white Americans robbing Africa and bombing Vietnam and doing ugly all over the world, causing hard times for Black folks and other colored people, she was glad not to be American. And when she watched the films about Africans fighting white folks so that hospitals and schools could be built for the kids, and the books about Fanny Lew somebody and Malcolm fighting for freedom, and the posters about the kids, kids littler than her even, studying and growing vegetables and all and the print saying how even kids were freedom fighters—she was proud not to be American. What she heard in school she pushed up against what was in her head. Then she started looking, just looking in the teacher's bloodshot eyes, looking at M'Dear's fat, looking at Dada Bibi's shiny skin, to decide just how she was going to arrange things in her head. It was simpler to watch than to listen.

"Ma Dear gone for the ambulance?" Horace in the doorway grinning, biting at the toast. "Old Freeny botch up the job? Next time I can take you to this nurse who—"

"Go to hell, nigger."

"Okay, okay," he said, closing his eyes and raising his hands like he wouldn't dream of pressing the magic number on nobody, would gladly take his pot of gold elsewhere. "But when that dead baby drops down and rips you open, don't yell for me to save ya. You'll bleed to death first."

Her sneaker missed his head by a fraction of an inch. And she sang real loud the Guinea-Bissau marching song the brother at the Center had taught her, to drown out his laughing. Her song ended as the door slammed. She eased into the mattress, not realizing she'd been tensed up and inches off the newspaper. Her body was sore with the clutching. She wanted to sleep, her eyes dry and stinging. She'd been afraid that if she blinked too long, she'd never open them again in life.

"To die for the people." Somebody in one of the films had said that. It had seemed okay to her at first. She tried to picture Pee Wee willing to die for the people. But all the pictures that came into her head about Pee Wee dying were mostly about Pee Wee and not the people. She tried to picture Horace standing up against the cops in the name of the kids, protecting Pee Wee maybe, or the other boys the pigs liked to beat up on. But it didn't exactly fit. She dreamed up another dude altogether. He looked a little like the brother in the film, only he was different cause he was hers. And he was blowing up police stations and running through the alleyways back of the projects, and she hiding him in her closet, sneaking him food from the kitchen. Was helping him load his guns to shoot the big businessmen with. And she was seeing him dragging through the streets, one leg shot off. And the President's special cops bending in the street to squeeze off the final bullet in his back. And she'd be holding his head in her lap, the blood trickling out of the side of his mouth, just like in the movies. But the pictures were no fun after a while.

So when Dada Bibi was rewinding, just looking at them, one at a time, but not pressing any discussion, Rae Ann'd said, "I want to live for the people." And Gretchen had said, "Right on." Wasn't nothin hip about dying. Then they started talking about what they could do with their lives to help Black people, to free Black people. And Gretchen said she didn't know if she'd feel like going to school long enough to teach, and she knew for sure she didn't feel like going back to the country so she couldn't see herself feeding nobody directly.

"Shit. I'm just here and ain't nobody gonna run no lame shit on me. Specially them teachers up at the school. Shit. That's the best I can do for the people, give them teachers hell. Shit," she added again, just to make clear no one had better ask her anything else about what she was prepared to do for her people.

"That's cool," said Dada Bibi, surprising them all. "Giving the teachers some static means you gotta hit them books, eat well, get plenty rest to keep the mind alert. Can't hit them with no lame shit, right?" She nodding to Gretchen.

"That's right," Gretchen said, her ass off her shoulders and her whole self trapped.

Rae Ann sniffled back a tear. She wasn't convinced she was really dying, but there was something righteous in the pain that came with thinking it. Something was wrong. She was being punished, that she knew. But she probably wasn't going to really die. She looked hard at the posters by the window, the wood carving she'd made for Kwanza on her desk, the map on the wall, the picture of Jesus on the closet she shared with her grandmother. She wasn't sure just who to make the promise to. So she simply addressed it to them all. If I can get through this time, she promised, I'm going to do something good. It left her dissatisfied, cold. To die for the people left her scared, mad, it wasn't fair. To live for the people left her confused, faintly inadequate. Was she up to it? And what?

"Here you go," M'Dear was saying, pitching the bag onto her bed. "Dinner be on in a minute."

What's wrong with me, she thought, M'Dear fraid to come in the room and get her slippers, fraid to come near me. What have I done? She up-ended the bag and set everything out neatly. A plan. She had to think methodically and stop all this crying and confusion. I will read everything two times. Then I'll know what to do. She allowed herself a moist blink. She would find out what she had done and take her whipping. Then everything would be like before. M'Dear would come into the room again and set awhile talking while she changed her shoes. Dada Bibi would hug her again. But then Dada Bibi would hug her no matter what. She even hugged the dirty kids from Mason Street. And drank behind them too without even rinsing the cup. Either Dada Bibi had a powerful health to combat germs, she thought, ripping open the packages, or the woman was crazy.

Witchbird

I

Curtains blew in and wrecked my whole dressing-table arrangement. Then in he came, eight kinds of darkness round his shoulders, this nutty bird screechin on his arm, on a nine-speed model, hand brakes and all. Said, "Come on, we goin ride right out of here just like you been wantin to for long time now." Patting the blanket lassoed to the carrier, leaning way back to do it, straddling the bike and thrusting his johnson out in front, patting, thrusting, insinuating. Bird doing a two-step on the handle bars.

Damn if I'm riding nowhere on some bike. I like trains. Am partial to fresh-smelling club cars with clear windows and cushy seats with white linen at the top for my cheek to snooze against. Not like the hulking, oil-leaking, smoke-belching monstrosity I came home on when the play closed. Leaning my cheek against the rattling windowpane, like to shook my teeth loose. Cigar stench, orange peels curling on the window sills, balls of wax paper greasy underfoot, the linen rank from umpteen different hair pomades. Want the trains like before, when I was little and the porter hauled me up by my wrists and joked with me about my new hat, earning the five my mama slipped him, leisurely. Watching out for my person, saving a sunny seat in the dining car, clearing the aisle of perverts from round my berth, making sure I was in the no-drama section of the train once we crossed the Potomac.

"Well, we can cross over to the other side," he saying, "you in a rut, girl, let's go." Leaning over the edge of the boat, trailing a hand in the blue-green Caribbean. No way. I like trains. Then uncorking the champagne, the bottle lodged between his thighs. Then the pop of the cork, froth cascading all over his lap. I tell you I'm partial to trains. "Well, all right," he sayin, stepping out his pants. "We go the way you want, any way you want. Cause you need a change," he saying, chuggin over my carpet in this bubble-top train he suddenly got. Bird shouting at me from the perch of eye-stinging white linen. And I know something gotta be wrong. Cause whenever I've asked for what I want in life, I never get it. So he got to be the devil or some kind of other ugly no-good thing.

"Get on out my room," I'm trying to say, jaws stuck. Whole right side and left paralyzed like I'm jammed in a cage. "You tromping on my house shoes and I don't play that. Them's the house shoes Heywood gave me for Mother's Day." Some joke. Heywood come up empty-handed every rent day, but that don't stop him from boarding all his ex ole ladies with me freebee. But yellow satin Hollywood slippers with pompoms on Mother's Day, figuring that's what I'm here for. Shit, I ain't nobody's mother. I'm a singer. I'm an actress. I'm a landlady look like. Hear me. Applaud me. Pay me.

"But look here," he saying, holding up a pair of house shoes even finer than mine. Holding em up around his ears like whatshisname, not the Sambo kid, the other little fellah. "Come on and take this ride with me."

All this talk about crossing over somewhere in dem golden slippers doing something to my arms. They jiggling loose from me like they through the bars of the cage, cept I know I'm under the covers in a bed, not a box. Just a jiggling. You'd think I was holding a hazel switch or a willow rod out in the woods witching for water. Peach twig better actually for locating subterranean springs. And I try to keep my mind on water, cause water is always a good thing. Creeks, falls, foundations, artesian wells. Baptism, candlelight ablutions, skinny-dipping in the lake, C&C with water on the side. The root of all worthy civilizations, water. Can heal you. Scrunched up under the quilts, the sick tray pushed to the side, the heal of rain washing against the window can heal you or make you pee the bed one, which'll wake you from fever, from sleep, will save you. Save me. Cause damn if this character ain't trying to climb into my berth. And if there's one thing I can do without, it's phantom fucking.

"Honey? You told me to wake you at dark. It's dark." Gayle, the brown-skin college girl my sometime piano player– sometime manager–mosttime friend Heywood dumped on me last time through here, jiggling my arms. Looking sorrowful about waking me up, she knows how sacred sleep can be, though not how scary.

"Here," she says, sliding my house shoes closer to the bed. "You know Heywood was all set to get you some tired old navy-blue numbers. I kept telling him you ain't nobody's grandma," she says, backing up to give me room to stretch, looking me over like she always does, comparing us I guess to flatter her own vanity, or wondering. maybe if it's possible

Heywood sees beyond friend, colleague, to maybe woman. All
the time trying to pry me open and check out is there some
long ago Heywood-me history. The truth is there's nothing to
tell. Heywood spot him a large, singing, easygoing type woman,
so he dumps his girl friends on me is all. I slide into the cold
slippers. They're too soft now and give no support. Cheap-ass
shoes. Here it is only Halloween, and they falling apart already.
I'm sucking my teeth but can't even hear myself good for the
caterwauling that damn bird's already set up in the woods,
tearing up the bushes, splitting twigs with the high notes. Bird
make me think some singer locked up inside, hostage. Cept
that bird ain't enchanting, just annoying.

"Laney's fixing a plate of supper for Miz Mary," Gayle is
saying, sliding a hand across my dressing-table scarf like she
dying to set her buns down and mess in my stuff. My make-up
kit ain't even unpacked, I'm noticing, and the play been closed
for over a month. I ain't even taken the time to review what
that role's done to my sense of balance, my sense of self. But
who's got time, what with all of Heywood's women cluttering
up my house, my life? Prancing around in shorty nightgowns
so I don't dare have company in. A prisoner in my own house.

"Laney say come on, she'll walk to the shop with you,
Honey. Me too. I think my number hit today. Maybe I can
help out with the bills."

Right. I'd settle for some privacy. Had such other plans for
my time right in through here. Bunch of books my nephew
sent untouched. Stacks of *Variety* unread under the kitchen
table. The new sheet music gathering dust on the piano. Been
wanting to go over the old songs, the ole Bessie numbers, Ma
Rainey, Trixie Smith, early Lena. So many women in them
songs waiting to be released into the air again, freed to roam.
Good time to be getting my new repertoire together too instead of rushing into my clothes and slapping my face together

just because Laney can't bear walking the streets alone after dark, and Gayle too scared to stay in the place by herself. Not that Heywood puts a gun to my head, but it's hard to say no to a sister with no place to go. So they wind up here, expecting me to absorb their blues and transform them maybe into songs. Been over a year since I've written any new songs. Absorbing, absorbing, bout to turn to mush rather than crystallize, sparkling.

II

Magazine lady on the phone this morning asked if I was boarding any new up-and-coming stars. Very funny. Vera, an early Heywood ex, had left here once her demo record was cut, went to New York and made the big time. Got me a part in the play, according to the phone voice contracted to do a four-page spread on Vera Willis, Star. But that ain't how the deal went down at all.

"I understand you used to room together" was how the phone interview started off. Me arranging the bottles and jars on my table, untangling the junk in my jewelry boxes. Remembering how Vera considered herself more guest than roommate, no problem whatsoever about leaving all the work to me, was saving herself for Broadway or Hollywood one. Like nothing I could be about was all that important so hey, Honey, pick up the mop. Me sitting on the piano bench waiting for Heywood to bring in a batch of cheat sheets, watching Vera in the yard with my nieces turning double dudge. Then Vera gets it in her mind to snatch away the rope and sing into the wooden handle, strolling, sassy, slinky between the dogwoods, taking poses, kicking at the tail of the rope and making teethy faces like Heywood taught her. The little girls stunned by this performance so like their own, only this one done brazenly, dead

serious, and by a grown-up lady slithering about the yard.
Staring out the window, I felt bad. I thought it was because
Vera was just not pretty. Not pretty and not nice. Obnoxious
in fact, selfish, vain, lazy. But yeah she could put a song over,
though she didn't have what you'd call musicianship. Like
she'd glide into a song, it all sounding quite dull normal at first.
Then a leg would shoot out as though from a split in some juicy
material kicking the mike cord out the way, then the song
would move somewhere. As though the spirit of music had
hovered cautious around her chin thinking it over, looking her
over, then liking that leg, swept into her mouth and took hold
of her throat and the song possessed her, electrified the leg,
sparked her into pretty. Later realizing I was staring at her,
feeling bad because of course she'd make it, have what she
wanted, go everywhere, meet everybody, be everything but
self-deserving.

First-class bitch was my two cents with the producers, just
to make it crystal clear I didn't intend riding in on her dress
tails but wanted to be judged by my own work, my reputation,
my audition. Don't nobody do me no favors, please, cause I'm
the baddest singer out here and one of the best character
actresses around. And just keeping warmed up till a Black script
comes my way.

Wasn't much of a part, but a good bit at the end. My
daddy used to instruct, if you can't be the star of the show,
aim for a good bit at the end. People remember that one
good line or that one striking piece of business by the bit
player in the third act. Well, just before the end, I come on
for my longest bit in the play. I'm carrying this veil, Vera's
mama's veil. The woman's so grief-stricken and whatnot, she
ain't even buttoned up right and forgot to put on her veil. So
here I come with the veil, and the mourners part the waves
to give me a path right to the grave site. But once I see the

coffin, my brown-sugar honey chile darlin dead and boxed, I forget all about the blood mama waiting for her veil. Forget all about maintaining my servant place in the bourgy household. I snatch off my apron and slowly lift that veil, for I am her true mother who cared for her and carried her through. I raise the hell outta that veil, transforming myself into Mother with a capital M. I let it drape slowly, slowly round my corn rolls, slowly lower it around my brow, my nose, mouth opening and the song bursting my jaws asunder as the curtain— well, not curtain, but the lights, cause we played it in the round, dim. Tore the play up with the song.

Course we did have a set-to about the costume. The designer saw my point—her talents were being squandered copying the pancake box. Playwright saw my point too, why distort a perfectly fine character just cause the director has mammy fantasies. An African patchwork apron was the only concession I'd make. Got to be firm about shit like that, cause if you ain't some bronze Barbie doll type or the big fro murder-mouth militant sister, you Aunt Jemima. Not this lady. No way. Got to fight hard and all the time with the scripts and the people. Cause they'll trap you in a fiction. Breath drained, heart stopped, vibrancy fixed, under arrest. Whole being entrapped, all possibility impaled, locked in some stereotype. And how you look trying to call from the box and be heard much less be understood long enough to get out and mean something useful and for real?

Sometimes I think I do a better job of it with the bogus scripts than with the life script. Fight harder with directors than with friends who trap me in their scenarios, put a drama on my ass. That's the problem with friends sometimes, they invest in who you were or seem to have been, capture you and you're through. Forget what you had in mind about changing, growing, developing. Got you typecasted. That's why I want some time off to think, to work up a new repertoire of songs, of life. So many women in them songs, in them streets, in me, waiting to be freed up.

Dozing, drifting into sleep sometime, the script sliding off the quilts into a heap, I hear folks calling to me. Calling from the box. Mammy Pleasant, was it? Tubman, slave women bundlers, voodoo queens, maroon guerrillas, combatant ladies in the Seminole nation, calls from the swamps, the tunnels, the classrooms, the studios, the factories, the roofs, from the doorway hushed or brassy in a dress way too short but it don't mean nuthin heavy enough to have to explain, just like Bad Bitch in the Sanchez play was saying. But then the wagon comes and they all rounded up and caged in the Bitch-Whore-Mouth mannequin with the dead eyes and the mothball breath, never to be heard from again. But want to sing a Harriet song and play a Pleasant role and bring them all center stage.

Wives weeping from the pillow not waking him cause he got his own weight to tote, wife in the empty road with one slipper on and the train not stopping, mother anxious with the needle and thread or clothespin as the children grow either much too fast to escape the attention of the posse or not fast enough to take hold. Women calling from the lock-up of the Matriarch cage. I want to put some of these new mother poems in those books the nephew sends to music. They got to be sung, hummed, shouted, chanted, swung.

Too many damn ransom notes fluttering in the window, or pitched in through the glass. Too much bail to post. Too many tunnels to dig and too much dynamite to set. I read the crazy scripts just to keep my hand in, cause I knew these newbreed Bloods going to do it, do it, do it. But meanwhile, I gotta work . . . and hell. Then read one of them books my nephew always sending and hearing the voices speaking free not calling from these new Black poems. Speaking free. So I know I ain't crazy.

But fast as we bust one, two loose, here come some crazy cracker throwing a croaker sack over Nat Turner's head, or white folks taking Malcolm hostage. And one time in Florida, dreaming in the hotel room about the Mary McLeod Bethune exhibit, I heard the woman calling from some diary entry they had under glass, a voice calling, muffled under the gas mask they clamped on hard and turned her on till she didn't know what was what. But calling for Black pages.

Then waking and trying to resume the reading, cept I can't remember just whom I'm supposed to try to animate in those dead, white pages I got to deal with till a Blood writes me my own. And catch myself calling to the white pages as I ripple them fast, listening to the pages for the entrapped voices calling, calling as the pages flutter.

Shit. It's enough to make you crazy. Where is my play, I wanna ask these new Bloods at the very next conference I hear about. Where the hell is my script? When I get to work my show?

"A number of scandalous rumors followed the run of the play, taking up an inordinate amount of space in the reviews," the lady on the phone was saying, me caught up in my own dialogue. "I understand most of the men connected with the play and Vera Willis had occasion to . . ."

There was Heywood, of course. Hadn't realized they'd gotten back together till that weekend we were packing the play off to New York. Me packing ahead of schedule and anxious to get out of D.C. fast, cause Bradwell, who used to manage the club where I been working for years, had invited me to his home for the weekend. For old times' sake, he'd said. Right. He'd married somebody else, a singer we used to crack on as I recall, not a true note in her, her tits getting her over. And now she'd left him rolling around lonely in the brownstone on

Edgecombe Avenue she'd once thought she just had to have. I went out and bought two hussy nightgowns. I was gonna break out in a whole new number. But never did work up the nerve. Never did have the occasion, ole Bradwell crying the blues about his wife. So what am I there for—to absorb, absorb, and transform if you can, ole girl. Absorb, absorb and try to convert it all to something other than fat.

Heywood calling to ask me to trade my suite near the theater for his room clear cross town.

"You can have both," I said, chuckling. "I'm off for the weekend."

"How come? Where you going?"

"Rendezvous. Remember the guy that used to own—"

"Cut the comedy. Where you going?"

"I'm telling you. I got a rendezvous with this gorgeous man I—"

"Look here," he cut in, "I'd invited Laney up to spend the weekend. That was before me and Vera got together again. I was wondering if you'd bail me out, maybe hang out with Laney till I can—"

"Heywood, you deaf? I just now told you I'm off to spend the—"

"Seriously?"

Made me so mad, I just hung up. Hung up and called me a fast cab.

III

Laney, Gayle, and me turn into Austin and run smack into a bunch of ghosts. Skeletons, pirates, and little devils with great flapping shopping bags set up a whirlwind around us. Laney spins around like in a speeded-up movie, holding Mary's dinner plate away from her dress and moaning, comically. Comically

175

at first. But then our bird friend in the woods starts shrieking and Laney moaning for real. Gayle empties her bag into one of the opened sacks, then leans in to retrieve her wallet, though I can't see why. All I got for the kids is a short roll of crumbly Lifesavers, hair with tobacco and lint from my trench coat lining. Screaming and wooo-wooooing, they jack-rabbit on down Austin. Then we heading past the fish truck, my mind on some gumbo, when suddenly Gayle stops. She heard it soon's I did. Laney still walking on till I guess some remark didn't get a uh-hunh and she turns around to see us way behind, Gayle's head cocked to the side.

"What it is?" Laney looking up and down the street for a clue. Other than the brother dumping the last of the ice from the fish truck and a few cats hysterical at the curb, too self-absorbed to launch a concerted attack on the truck, there ain't much to keep the eyes alive. "What?" Laney whispers.

From back of the houses we hear some mother calling her son, the voice edgy on the last syllable, getting frantic. Probably Miz Baker, whose six-foot twelve-year-old got a way of scooting up and down that resembles too much the actions of a runaway bandit to the pigs around here. Mainly, he got the outlaw hue, and running too? Shit, Miz Baker stay frantic. The boy answers from the woods, which starts the bird up again, screeching, ripping through the trees, like she trying to find a way out of them woods and heaven help us if she do, cause she dangerous with rage.

"That him?" Gayle asks, knowing I'm on silence this time of night.

"Who?" Laney don't even bother looking at me, cause she knows I got a whole night of singing and running off at the mouth to get through once Mary lets me out from under the dryer and I get to the club. "Witchbird?" Laney takes a couple steps closer to us. "Yawl better tell me what's up," she says, "cause this here gettin spoooo-keeee!"

It's mostly getting dark and Laney don't wanna have to take the shortcut through the woods. Witchbird gotta way of screaming on you sudden, scare the shit outta you. Laney trying to balance that plate of dinner and not lose the juice. She is worried you can tell, and not just about Mary's mouth over cold supper. Laney's face easy to read, everything surfaces to the skin. Dug that the day Heywood brought her by. She knew she was being cut loose, steered safely to cove, the boat shoving off and bye, baby, bye. Sad crinkling round the eyes, purples under the chin, throat pulsating. Gayle harder to read, a Scorpio, she plays it close to the chest unless she can play it for drama.

"Tell me, Gayle. What it is?"

"Heywood back in town."

"Ohhh, girl, don't tell me that." Laney takes a coupla sideways steps, juggling the plate onto one hand so she can tug down the jersey she barmaids in. "You better come on."

"You know one thing," Gayle crooning it, composing a monologue, sound like. "There was a time when that laugh could turn me clear around in the street and make me forget just where I thought I was going." On cue, Heywood laughs one of his laughs and Gayle's head tips, locating his whereabouts. She hands me her suede bag heavy with the pic comb and the schoolbooks. It's clear she fixin to take off. "I really loved that dude," she saying, theatrics gone. Laney moves on, cause she don't want to hear nuthin about Heywood and especially from Gayle. "He gets his thing off," Laney had said to Gayle the night she was dumped, "behind the idea of his harem sprawled all over Honey's house gassing about him. I refuse," she had said and stuck to it.

"I really, really did," Gayle saying, something leaking in her voice.

Laney hears it and steps back. It's spilling on her shoes, her dress, soaking into her skin. She moves back again cause Gayle's zone is spreading. Gayle so filling up and brimming over, she gotta take over more and more room to accommodate the swell. Her leaking splashes up against me too—Heywood taking a solo, teeth biting out a rhythm on the back of his lower lip, Heywood at the wheel leaning over for a kiss fore he cranks up, Heywood wound up in rumpled sheets with his cap pulled down, sweat beading on his nose, waiting on breakfast, Heywood doing the dance of the hot hands and Gayle scrambling for a potholder to catch the coffeepot he'd reached for with his fool self, Heywood falling off the porch and Gayle's daddy right on him. Gayle's waves wash right up on me and I don't want no parts of it. Let it all wash right through me, can't use it, am to the brim with my own stuff waiting to be transformed. Washes through me so fast the pictures blur and all I feel is heat and sparks. And then I hear the laugh again.

"Oh, shit," Laney says, watching the hem of Gayle's dress turning into the alley. "That girl is craaaaa-zeee, ya heah?" Her legs jiggling to put her in the alley in more ways than one, but that plate leaking pot likker and demanding its due.

Bright's strung up lights in the alley and you can make him out clear, hunched over the bathtub swishing barbeque sauce with a sheet-wrapped broom. Cora visible too, doing a shonuff flower arrangement on the crushed ice with the watermelon slices. And there's Heywood, ole lanky Heywood in his cap he says Babs Gonzales stole from Kenny Clarke and he in turn swiped from Babs. One arm lazy draped around Gayle's shoulders, the other crooked in the fence he lounges against, sipping some of Bright's bad brandy brew, speakeasy style. Other folks around the card table sipping from jelly jars or tin cups. But

Heywood would have one of Cora's fine china numbers. He's looking good.

"What's goin on?" Laney asks in spite of herself, but refuses to move where she can see into the yard. All she got to do is listen, cause Heywood is the baritone lead of the eight-part card game opus.

"Ho!"

"Nigger, just play the card."

"Gonna. Gonna do that direckly. Right on yawl's ass."

"Do it to em, Porter."

"Don't tell him nuthin. He don't wanna know nuthin. He ain't never been nuthin but a fool."

Porter spits on the card and slaps it on his forehead.

"Got the bitch right here"—he's pointing—"the bitch that's gonna set ya."

"Nigger, you nasty, you know that? You a nasty-ass nigger and that's why don't nobody never wanna play with yo nasty-ass self."

"Just play the card, Porter."

"Ho!" He bangs the card down with a pop and the table too.

"Iz you crazy?"

"If Porter had any sense, he'd be dangerous."

"Sense enough to send these blowhards right out the back door. Ho!"

"You broke the table and the ashtray, fool."

"And that was my last cigarette too. Gimme a dollar."

"Dollar! I look like a fool? If you paying Bright a dollar for cigarettes, you the fool."

"I want the dollar for some barbeque."

"What! What!" Porter sputtering and dancing round the yard. "How come I gotta replace one cigarette with a meal?"

"Okay then, buy some watermelon and some of the fire juice."

"You don't logic, man. You sheer don't logic. All I owe you is a cigarette."

"What about the table?"

"It ain't your table, nigger."

Laney is click-clicking up the street, giving wide berth to the path that leads through the woods. "Why Gayle want to put herself through them changes all over again," she is mumbling, grinding her heels in the broken pavement, squashing the dandelions. "I wouldn't put myself through none of that mess again for all the money." She picking up speed and I gotta trot to catch up. "I don't know how you can stay friends with a man like that, Honey."

"He don't do me no harm," I say, then mad to break my silence.

"Oh, no?" She trying to provoke me into debating it, so she says it again, "Oh, no?"

I don't want to get into this, all I want is to get into Mary's shampoo chair, to laze under Mary's hands and have her massage all the hurt out of my body, tension emulsified in the coconut-oil suds, all fight sprayed away. My body been so long on chronic red alert messin with them theater folks, messing with stock types, real types, messing with me, I need release, not hassles.

"You think it's no harm the way he uses you, Honey? What are you, his mother, his dumping grounds? Why you put up with it? Why you put up with us, with me? Oh, Honey, I—"

I walk right along, just like she ain't talking to me. I can't take in another thing.

IV

"Well, all right! Here she come, Broadway star," someone bellows at me as the bell over the door jangles.

Witchbird

"Come on out from under that death, Honey," Mary says soon's we get halfway in the door. "Look like you sportin a whole new look in cosmetics. Clown white, ain't it? Or is it Griffin All White applied with a putty knife?" Mary leaves her customer in the chair to come rip the wig off my head. "And got some dead white woman on your head too. Why you wanna do this to yourself, Honey? You auditioning for some zombie movie?"

"Protective covering," Bertha says, slinging the magazine she'd been reading onto the pile. "You know how Honey likes to put herself out of circulation, Mary. Honey, you look like one of them creatures Nanna Mae raised from the dead. What they do to you in New York, girl? We thought you'd come back tired, but not embalmed."

"Heard tell a duppy busted up some posh do on the hill last Saturday," Mary's customer saying. "Lotta zombies round here."

"Some say it was the ghost of Willie Best come back to kill him somebody."

"Long's it's some white somebody, okay by me."

"Well, you know colored folks weren't exactly kind to the man when he was alive. Could be—"

"Heard Heywood's back on the scene," Bertha comes over to say to me. She lifts my hand off the armrest and checks my manicure and pats my hand to make up for, I guess, her not-so-warm greeting. "Be interesting to see just what kinda bundle he gonna deposit on your doorstep this time." Laney cuts her eye at Bertha, surrenders up the juiceless meal and splits. "Like you ain't got nuthin better to do with ya tits but wet-nurse his girls."

I shove Bertha's hand off mine and stretch out in my favorite chair. Mary's got a young sister now to do the scratchin and hot oil. She parts hair with her fingers, real gentle-like. Feels good. I'm whipped. I think on all I want to do with the new music and I'm feelin crowded, full up, rushed.

"No use you trying to ig me, Honey," Bertha says real loud. "Cause I'm Mary's last customer. We got all night."

"Saw Frieda coming out the drugstore," somebody is saying. "Package looked mighty interesting."

Everybody cracking up, Bertha too. I ease my head back and close my eyes under the comb scratching up dandruff.

"Obviously Ted is going on the road again and Frieda gonna pack one of her famous box snacks."

"Got the recipe for the oatmeal cookies richeah," someone saying. "One part rolled oats, one long drip of sorghum, fistful of raisins, and a laaaarge dose of saltpeter."

"Salt pete–er salt pete–er," somebody singing through the nose, outdoing Dizzy.

"Whatchu say!"

"Betcha there'll be plenty straaange mashed potatoes on the table tonight."

The young girl's rubbin is too hard in the part and the oil too hot. But she so busy cracking up, she don't notice my ouchin.

"Saltpetertaters, what better dish to serve a man going on the road for three days. Beats calling him every hour on the half-hour telling him to take a cold shower."

"Best serve him with a summons for being so downright ugly. Can't no woman be really serious about messin with Ted, he too ugly."

"Some that looks ugly . . ." Couldn't catch the rest of it, but followed the giggling well enough after what sounded like a second of silence.

"Mary"—someone was breathless with laughter—"when you and the sisters gonna give another one of them balls?"

"Giiirl," howls Bertha, "Wasn't that ball a natural ball?"

V

Bertha and Mary and me organized this Aquarian Ball. We so busy making out the lists, hooking people up, calling in some new dudes from the Islands just to jazz it up, hiring musicians and all, we clean forgot to get me an escort. I'd just made Marshall the trumpet player give me back my key cause all he ever wanted to do was bring by a passle of fish that needed cleaning and frying, and I was sick of being cook and confidante. I bet if I lost weight, people'd view me different. Other than Marshall, wasn't no man on the horizon, much less the scene. Mary, me and Bertha playing bid whist and I feel a Boston in my bones, so ain't paying too much attention to the fact that this no escort status of mine is serious business as far as Bertha's concerned.

"What about Heywood?" she says, scooping up the kitty.

Right on cue as always, in comes ole lanky Heywood with his cap yanked down around his brow and umpteen scarves around his mouth looking like Jesse James. He's got a folio of arrangements to deliver to me, but likes to make a big production first of saying hello to sisters. So while he's doing his rhyming couplets and waxing lyric and whatnot, I'm looking him over, trying to unravel my feelings about this man I've known, worked with, befriended for so long. Good manager, never booked me in no dumps. Always sees to it that the money ain't funny. A good looker and all, but always makes me feel more mother or older sister, though he four months to the day older than me. Naaw, I conclude, Heywood just my buddy. But I'm thinking too that I need a new buddy, cause he's got me bagged somehow. Put me in a bag when I wasn't looking. Folks be sneaky with their scenarios and secret casting.

"Say, handsome," Bertha say, jumping right on it, "ain't you taking Honey here to the ball?"

"Why somebody got to take her? I thought yawl was giving it."

"That ain't no answer. Can't have Honey waltzin in with-out—"

"Hold on," he saying, unwrapping the scarves cause we got the oven up high doing the meat patties.

"Never mind all that," says Mary. "Who you know can do it? Someone nice now."

"Well, I'll tell you," he says, stretching his arm around me. "I don't know no men good enough for the queen here."

"You a drag and a half," says Bertha.

"And I don't want to block traffic either," he says. "I mean if Honey comes in with my fine self on her arm, no man there is—"

"Never mind that," says Mary, slapping down an ace. "What about your friends, I'm askin you?"

"Like I said, I don't know anybody suitable."

"What you mean is, you only knows the ladies," says Bertha, disgusted. "You the type dude that would probably come up with a basket case for escort anyway. Club foot, hunchback, palsied moron or something. Just to make sure Honey is still available for you to mammify."

"Now wait a minute," he says, rising from the chair and pushing palms against the air like he fending us off. "How I get involved in yawl's arrangements?"

"You a friend, ain't ya? You a drag, that's for sure." Bertha lays down her hand, we thought to hit Heywood, come to find she trump tight.

Heywood puts the folio in my lap and rewraps the scarves for take-off, and we spend the afternoon being sullen, and damn near burnt up the meat patties.

"I'm getting tired of men like that," grumbles Bertha after while. "Either it's 'Hey, Mama, hold my head,' or 'Hey, Sister,' at three in the morning. When it get to be 'Sugar Darling'? I'm tired of it. And you, Honey, should be the tiredest of all."

"So I just took my buns right to her house, cause she my friend and what else a friend for?" one of the women is saying. Mary's easing my head back on the shampoo tray, so I can't see who's talking.

"So did you tell her?"

"I surely did. I held her by the shoulders and said, 'Helen, you do know that Amos is on the dope now, don't you?' And she kinda went limp in my arms like she was gonna just crumble and not deal with it."

"A myth all that stuff about our strength and strength and then some," Bertha saying.

" 'If Amos blow his mind now, who gonna take care of you in old age, Helen?' I try to tell her."

"So what she say?"

"She don't say nuthin. She just cry."

"It's a hellafyin thing. No jobs, nary a fit house in sight, famine on the way, but the dope just keep comin and comin."

I don't know Helen or Amos. Can't tell whether Amos is the son or the husband. Ain't that a bitch. But I feel bad inside. I crumple up too hearing it. Picturing a Helen seeing her Amos in a heap by the bathtub, gagging, shivering, defeated, not like he should be. Getting the blankets to wrap him up, holding him round, hugging him tight, rocking, rocking, rocking.

"You need a towel?" Mary whispers, bending under the dryer. No amount of towel's gonna stop the flood, I'm thinking. I don't even try to stop. Let it pour, let it get on out so I can travel light. I'm thinking maybe I'll do Billie's number tonight. Biting my lip and trying to think on the order of songs

I'm going to get through this evening and where I can slip Billie in.

"What's with you, Honey?"

"Mary got this damn dryer on KILL," I say, and know I am about to talk myself hoarse and won't be fit for singing.

CHRISTMAS EVE AT JOHNSON'S DRUGS N GOODS

I was probably the first to spot them cause I'd been watching the entrance to the store on the lookout for my daddy, knowing that if he didn't show soon, he wouldn't be coming at all. His new family would be expecting him to spend the holidays with them. For the first half of my shift, I'd raced the cleaning cart down the aisles doing a slapdash job on the signs and glass cages, eager to stay in view of the doorway. And look like Johnson's kept getting bigger, swelling, sprawling itself all over the corner lot, just to keep me from the door, to wear me out in the marathon vigil.

In point of fact, Johnson's Drugs N Goods takes up less than one-third of the block. But it's laid out funny in crisscross aisles so you get to feeling like a rat in an endless maze. Plus the ceilings are high and the fluorescents a blazing white. And Mrs. Johnson's got these huge signs sectioning off the spaces— TOBACCO   DRUGS   HOUSEWARES, etc.—like it was some big-time department store. The thing is, till the two noisy women came in, it felt like a desert under a blazing sun. Piper in Tobacco even had on shades. The new dude in Drugs looked like he was at the end of a wrong-way telescope. I got to feeling like a nomad with the cleaning cart, trekking across the sands with no end in sight, wandering. The overhead lights creating mirages and racing up my heart till I'd realize that wasn't my daddy in the parking lot, just the poster-board Santa Claus. Or that wasn't my daddy in the entrance way, just the Burma Shave man in a frozen stance. Then I'd tried to make out pictures of Daddy getting off the bus at the terminal, or driving a rented car past the Chamber of Commerce building, or sitting jammed-leg in one of them DC point-o-nine brand X planes, coming to see me.

By the time the bus pulled into the lot and the two women in their big-city clothes hit the door, I'd decided Daddy was already at the house waiting for me, knowing that for a mirage too, since Johnson's is right across from the railroad and bus terminals and the house is a dollar-sixty cab away. And I know he wouldn't feature going to the house on the off chance of running into Mama. Or even if he escaped that fate, having to sit in the parlor with his hat in his lap while Aunt Harriet looks him up and down grunting, too busy with the latest crossword puzzle contest to offer the man some supper. And Uncle Henry talking a blue streak bout how he outfoxed the city council or somethin and nary a cold beer in sight for my daddy.

But then the two women came banging into the store and I felt better. Right away the store stopped sprawling, got fixed. And we all got pulled together from our various zones to one focal point—them. Changing up the whole atmosphere of the place fore they even got into the store proper. Before we knew it, we were all smiling, looking halfway like you supposed to on Christmas Eve, even if you do got to work for ole lady Johnson, who don't give you no slack whatever the holiday.

"What the hell does this mean, Ethel?" the one in the fur coat say, talking loud and fast, yanking on the rails that lead the way into the store. "What are we, cattle? Being herded into the blankety-blank store and in my fur coat," she grumbles, boosting herself up between the rails, swinging her body along like the kids do in the park.

Me and Piper look at each other and smile. Then Piper moves down to the edge of the counter right under the Tobacco sign so as not to miss nothing. Madeen over in Housewares waved to me to ask what's up and I just shrug. I'm fascinated by the women.

"Look here," the one called Ethel say, drawing the words out lazy slow. "Do you got a token for this sucker?" She's shoving hard against the turnstile folks supposed to exit through. Pushing past and grunting, the turnstile crank cranking like it gonna bust, her Christmas corsage of holly and bells just ajingling and hanging by a thread. Then she gets through and stumbles toward the cigar counter and leans back against it, studying the turnstile hard. It whips back around in place, making scrunching noises like it's been abused.

"You know one thing," she say, dropping her face onto her coat collar so Piper'd know he's being addressed.

"Ma'am?"

"That is one belligerent bad boy, that thing right there."

Piper laughs his prizewinning laugh and starts touching the stacks of gift-wrapped stuff, case the ladies in the market for pipe tobacco or something. Two or three of the customers who'd been falling asleep in the magazines coming to life now, inching forward. Phototropism, I'd call it, if somebody asked me for a word.

The one in the fur coat's coming around now the right way —if you don't count the stiff-elbow rail-walking she was doing

—talking about "Oh, my God, I can walk, I can walk, Ethel, praise de lawd."

The two women watching Piper touch the cigars, the humidors, the gift-wrapped boxes. Mostly he's touching himself, cause George Lee Piper love him some George Lee Piper. Can't blame him. Piper be fine.

"You work on commissions, young man?" Fur Coat asking.

"No, ma'am."

The two women look at each other. They look over toward the folks inching forward. They look at me gliding by with the cleaning cart. They look back at each other and shrug.

"So what's his problem?" Ethel says in a stage whisper. "Why he so hot to sell us something?"

"Search me." Fur Coat starts flapping her coat and frisking herself. "You know?" she asking me.

"It's a mystery to me," I say, doing my best to run ole man Samson over. He sneaking around trying to jump Madeen in Housewares. And it is a mystery to me how come Piper always so eager to make a sale. You'd think he had half interest in the place. He says it's because it's his job, and after all, the Johnsons are Black folks. I guess so, I guess so. Me, I just clean the place and stay busy in case Mrs. J is in the prescription booth, peeking out over the top of the glass.

When I look around again, I see that the readers are suddenly very interested in cigars. They crowding around Ethel and Fur Coat. Piper kinda embarrassed by all the attention, though fine as he is, he oughta be used to it. His expression's cool but his hands give him away, sliding around the counter like he shuffling a deck of slippery cards. Fur Coat nudges Ethel and they bend over to watch the hands, doing these chicken-head jerkings. The readers take up positions just like a director was hollering "Places" at em. Piper, never one to disappoint an audience, starts zipping around these invisible walnut shells. Right away Fur Coat whips out a little red change purse and slaps a dollar bill on the counter. Ethel dips deep into her coat pocket, bending her knees and being real comic, then plunks down some change. Ole man Sampson tries to boost up on my cleaning cart to see the shells that ain't there.

"Scuse me, Mr. Sampson," I say, speeding the cart up sudden so that quite naturally he falls off, the dirty dog.

Piper is snapping them imaginary shells around like nobody's business, one of the readers leaning over another's shoulder, staring pop-eyed.

"All right now, everybody step back," Ethel announces. She waves the crowd back and pushes up one coat sleeve, lifts her fist into the air and jerks out one stiff finger from the bunch, and damn if the readers don't lift their heads to behold in amazement this wondrous finger.

"That, folks," Fur Coat explains, "is what is known as the indicator finger. The indicator is about to indicate the indicatee."

"Say wha?" Dirty ole man Sampson decides he'd rather sneak up on Madeen than watch the show.

"What's going on over there?" Miz Della asks me. I spray the watch case and make a big thing of wiping it and ignoring her. But then the new dude in Drugs hollers over the same thing.

"Christmas cheer gone to the head. A coupla vaudevillians," I say. He smiles, and Miz Della says "Ohhh" like I was talking to her.

"This one," Ethel says, planting a finger exactly one-quarter of an inch from the countertop.

Piper dumb-shows a lift of the shell, turning his face away as though he can't bear to look and find the elusive pea ain't there and he's gonna have to take the ladies' money. Then his

191

eyes swivel around and sneak a peek and widen, lighting up his whole face in a prizewinning grin.

"You got it," he shouts.

The women grab each other by the coat shoulders and jump each other up and down. And I look toward the back cause I know Mrs. J got to be hearing all this carrying-on, and on payday if Mr. J ain't handing out the checks, she's going to give us some long lecture about decorum and what it means to be on board at Johnson's Drugs N Goods. I wheel over to the glass jars and punch bowls, wanting alibi distance just in case. And also to warn Madeen about Sampson gaining on her. He's ducking down behind the coffeepots, walking squat and shameless.

"Pay us our money, young man," Fur Coat is demanding, rapping her knuckles on the counter.

"Yeah, what kind of crooked shell game is you running here in this joint?" say Ethel, finding a good foil character to play.

"We should hate to have to turn the place out, young man."

"It out," echoes Ethel.

The women nod to the crowd and a coupla folks giggle. And Piper tap-taps on the cash register like he shonuff gonna give em they money. I'd rather they turned the place out myself. I want to call my daddy. Only way any of us are going to get home in time to dress for the Christmas dance at the center is for the women to turn it out. Like I say, Piper ain't too clear about the worker's interest versus management's, as the dude in Drugs would say it. So he's light-tapping and quite naturally the cash drawer does not come out. He's yanking some unseen dollar from the not-there drawer and handing it over. Damn if Fur Coat don't snatch it, deal out the bills to herself and her friend and then make a big production out of folding the money flat and jamming it in that little red change purse.

"I wanna thank you," Ethel says, strolling off, swinging her pocketbook so that the crowd got to back up and disperse. Fur Coat spreads her coat and curtsies.

"A pleasure to do business with you ladies," Piper says, tipping his hat, looking kinda disappointed that he didn't sell em something. Tipping his hat the way he tipped the shells, cause you know Mrs. J don't allow no hats indoors. I came to work in slacks one time and she sent me home to change and docked me too. I wear a gele some times just to mess her around, and you can tell she trying to figure out if she'll go for it or not. The woman is crazy. Not Uncle Henry type crazy, but Black property owner type crazy. She thinks this is a museum, which is why folks don't hardly come in here to shop. That's okay cause we all get to know each other well. It's not okay cause it's a drag to look busy. If you look like you ain't buckling under a weight of work, Mrs. J will have you count the Band-Aids in the boxes to make sure the company ain't pulling a fast one. The woman crazy.

Now Uncle Henry type crazy is my kind of crazy. The type crazy to get you a job. He march into the "saloon" as he calls it and tells Leon D that he is not an equal opportunity employer and that he, Alderman Henry Peoples, is going to put some fire to his ass. So soon's summer comes, me and Madeen got us a job at Leon D. Salon. One of them hushed, funeral type shops with skinny models parading around for customers corseted and strangling in their seats, huffin and puffin.

Madeen got fired right off on account of the pound of mascara she wears on each lash and them weird dresses she designs for herself (with less than a yard of cloth each if you ask me). I did my best to hang in there so's me and Madeen'd have hang-around money till Johnson started hiring again. But it was hard getting back and forth from the stockroom to this little kitchen to fix the espresso to the showroom. One minute up to your ass in carpet, the next skidding across white linoleum, the next making all this noise on ceramic tile and people looking around at you and all. Was there for two weeks and just about had it licked by stationing different kind of shoes at each place that I could slip into, but then Leon D stumbled over my bedroom slippers one afternoon.

But to hear Uncle Henry tell it, writing about it all to Daddy, I was working at a promising place making a name for myself. And Aunt Harriet listening to Uncle Henry read the letter, looking me up and down and grunting. She know what kind of name it must be, cause my name in the family is Miss Clumsy. Like if you got a glass-top coffee table with doodads on em, or a hurricane lamp sitting on a mantel anywhere near a door I got to come through, or an antique jar you brought all the way from Venice the time you won the crossword puzzle contest—you can rest assure I'll demolish them by and by. I ain't vicious, I'm just clumsy. It's my gawky stage, Mama says. Aunt Harriet cuts her eye at Mama and grunts.

My daddy advised me on the phone not to mention anything to the Johnsons about this gift of mine for disaster or the fact that I worked at Leon D. Salon. No sense the Johnson's calling up there to check on me and come to find I knocked over a perfume display two times in the same day. Like I say—it's a gift. So when I got to clean the glass jars and punch bowls at Johnson's, I take it slow and pay attention. Then I take up my station relaxed in Fabrics, where the worst that can happen is I upset a box of pins.

Mrs. J is in the prescription booth, and she clears her throat real loud. We all look to the back to read the smoke signals. She ain't paying Fur Coat and Ethel no attention. They over in Cosmetics messing with Miz Della's mind and her customers. Mrs. J got her eye on some young teen-agers browsing around Jewelry. The other eye on Piper. But this does not mean Piper is supposed to check the kids out. It means Madeen is. You got to know how to read Mrs. J to get along.

She always got one eye on Piper. Tries to make it seem like she don't trust him at the cash register. That may be part of the reason now, now that she's worked up this cover story so in her mind. But we all know why she watches Piper, same reason we all do. Cause Piper is so fine you just can't help yourself. Tall and built up, blue-black and smooth, got the nerve to have dimples, and wears this splayed-out push-broom mustache he's always raking in with three fingers. Got a big butt too that makes you wanna hug the customer that asks for the cartoons Piper keeps behind him, two shelfs down. Mercy. And when it's slow, or when Mrs. J comes bustling over for the count, Piper steps from behind the counter and shows his self. You get to see the whole Piper from the shiny boots to the glistening fro and every inch of him fine. Enough to make you holler.

Miz Della in Cosmetics, a sister who's been passing for years but fooling nobody but herself, she always lolligagging over to Tobacco talking bout are there any new samples of those silver-tipped cigars for women. Piper don't even squander energy to bump her off any more. She mostly just ain't even there. At first he would get mad when she used to act hinkty and had these white men picking her up at the store. Then he got sorrowful about it all, saying she was a pitiful person. Now that she's going out with the blond chemist back there, he just wiped her off the map. She tries to mess with him, but Piper ain't heard the news she's been born. Sometimes his act slips, though, cause he does take a lot of unnecessary energy to play up to Madeen whenever Miz Della's hanging around. He's not consistent in his attentions, and that spurs Madeen the dress designer to madness. And Piper really oughta put brakes on that, cause Madeen subject to walk in one day in a fishnet dress and no underwear and then what he goin do about that?

Last year on my birthday my daddy got on us about dressing like hussies to attract the boys. Madeen shrugged it off and went about her business. It hurt my feelings. The onliest reason I was wearing that tight sweater and that skimpy skirt was cause I'd been to the roller rink and that's how we dress. But my daddy didn't even listen and I was really hurt. But then later that night, I come through the living room to make some cocoa and he apologized. He lift up from the couch where he always sleeps when he comes to visit, lifted up and whispered it—"Sorry." I could just make him out by the light from the refrigerator.

"Candy," he calls to make sure I heard him. And I don't want to close the frig door cause I know I'll want to remember this scene, figuring it's going to be the last birthday visit cause he fixin to get married and move outta state.

"Sir?"

He pat the couch and I come on over and just leave the frig door open so we can see each other. I forgot to put the milk down, so I got this cold milk bottle in my lap, feeling stupid.

"I was a little rough on you earlier," he say, picking something I can't see from my bathrobe. "But you're getting to be a woman now and certain things have to be said. Certain things have to be understood so you can decide what kind of woman you're going to be, ya know?"

"Sir," I nod. I'm thinking Aunt Harriet ought to tell me, but then Aunt Harriet prefers to grunt at folks, reserving words for the damn crossword puzzles. And my mama stay on the road so much with the band, when she do come home for a hot minute all she has to tell me is "My slippers're in the back closet" or "Your poor tired Ma'd like some coffee."

He takes my hand and don't even kid me about the milk bottle, just holds my hand for a long time saying nothing, just squeezes it. And I know he feeling bad about moving away and

196

all, but what can he do, he got a life to lead. Just like Mama
got her life to lead. Just like I got my life to lead and'll probably
leave here myself one day and become an actress or a director.
And I know I should tell him it's all right. Sitting there with
that milk bottle chilling me through my bathrobe, the light
from the refrigerator throwing funny shadows on the wall, I
know that years later when I'm in trouble or something, or hear
that my daddy died or something like that, I'm going feel real
bad that I didn't tell him—it's all right, Daddy, I understand.
It ain't like he'd made any promises about making a home for
me with him. So it ain't like he's gone back on his word. And
if the new wife can't see taking in no half-grown new daughter,
hell, I understand that. I can't get the words together, neither
can he. So we just squeeze each other's hands. And that'll have
to do.

"When I was a young man," he says after while, "there were
girls who ran around all made up in sassy clothes. And they
were okay to party with, but not the kind you cared for, ya
know?" I nod and he pats my hand. But I'm thinking that ain't
right, to party with a person you don't care for. How come you
can't? I want to ask, but he's talking. And I was raised not to
interrupt folk when they talking, especially my daddy. "You
and Madeen cause quite a stir down at the barbershop." He
tries to laugh it, but it comes out scary. "Got to make up your
mind now what kind of woman you're going to be. You know
what I'm saying?" I nod and he loosens his grip so I can go
make my cocoa.

I'm messing around in the kitchenette feeling dishonest.
Things I want to say, I haven't said. I look back over toward
the couch and know this picture is going to haunt me later.
Going to regret the things left unsaid. Like a coward, like a
child maybe. I fix my cocoa and keep my silence, but I do
remember to put the milk back and close the refrigerator door.

"Candy?"

"Sir?" I'm standing there in the dark, the frig door closed now and we can't even see each other.

"It's not about looks anyway," he says, and I hear him settling deep into the couch and pulling up the bedclothes. "And it ain't always about attracting some man either . . . not necessarily."

I'm waiting to hear what it is about, the cup shaking in the saucer and me wanting to ask him all over again how it was when he and Mama first met in Central Park, and how it used to be when they lived in Philly and had me and how it was when the two of them were no longer making any sense together but moved down here anyway and then split up. But I could hear that breathing he does just before the snoring starts. So I hustle on down the hall so I won't be listening for it and can't get to sleep.

All night I'm thinking about this woman I'm going to be. I'll look like Mama but don't wanna be no singer. Was named after Grandma Candestine but don't wanna be no fussy old woman with a bunch of kids. Can't see myself turning into Aunt Harriet either, doing crossword puzzles all day long. I look over at Madeen, all sprawled out in her bed, tangled up in the sheets looking like the alcoholic she trying to be these days, sneaking liquor from Uncle Henry's closet. And I know I don't wanna be stumbling down the street with my boobs out and my dress up and my heels cracking off and all. I write for a whole hour in my diary trying to connect with the future me and trying not to hear my daddy snoring.

Fur Coat and Ethel in Housewares talking with Madeen. I know they must be cracking on Miz Della, cause I hear Madeen saying something about equal opportunity. We used to say that Mrs. J was an equal opportunity employer for hiring

Miz Della. But then she went and hired real white folks—a blond, crew-cut chemist and a pimply-face kid for the stockroom. If you ask me, that's running equal opportunity in the ground. And running the business underground cause don't nobody round here deal with no white chemist. They used to wrinkly old folks grinding up the herbs and bark and telling them very particular things to do and not to do working the roots. So they keep on going to Mama Drear down past the pond or Doc Jessup in back of the barbershop. Don't do a doctor one bit of good to write out a prescription talking about fill it at Johnson's, cause unless it's an emergency folk stay strictly away from a white root worker, especially if he don't tell you what he doing.

Aunt Harriet in here one day when Mama Drear was too sick to counsel and quite naturally she asks the chemist to explain what all he doing back there with the mortar and pestle and the scooper and the scales. And he say something about rules and regulations, the gist of which was mind your business, lady. Aunt Harriet dug down deep into her crossword-puzzle words and pitched a natural bitch. Called that man a bunch of choicest names. But the line that got me was—"Medication without explanation is obscene." And what she say that for, we ran that in the ground for days. Infatuation without fraternization is obscene. Insemination without obligation is tyranny. Fornication without contraception is obtuse, and so forth and so on. Madeen's best line came out the night we were watching a TV special about welfare. Sterilization without strangulation and hell's damnation is I-owe-you-one-crackers. Look like every situation called for a line like that, and even if it didn't, we made it fit.

Then one Saturday morning we were locked out and we standing around shivering in our sweaters and this old white dude jumps out a pickup truck hysterical, his truck still in gear and backing out the lot. His wife had given their child an overdose of medicine and the kid was out cold. Look like everything he said was grist for the mill.

"She just administered the medicine without even reading the label," he told the chemist, yanking on his jacket so the man couldn't even get out his keys. "She never even considered the fact it might be dangerous, the medicine so old and all." We follow the two down the aisle to the prescription booth, the old white dude talking a mile a minute, saying they tried to keep the kid awake, tried to walk him, but he wouldn't walk. Tried to give him an enema, but he wouldn't stay propped up. Could the chemist suggest something to empty his stomach out and sooth his inflamed ass and what all? And besides he was breathing funny and should he administer mouth-to-mouth resuscitation? The minute he tore out of there and ran down the street to catch up with his truck, we started in.

Administration without consideration is illiterate. Irrigation without resuscitation is evacuation without ambulation is inflammation without information is execution without restitution is. We got downright silly about the whole thing till Mrs. J threatened to fire us all. But we kept it up for a week.

Then the new dude in Drugs who don't never say much stopped the show one afternoon when we were trying to figure out what to call the street riots in the sixties and so forth. He say Revolution without Transformation is Half-assed. Took me a while to ponder that one, a whole day in fact just to work up to it. After while I would listen real hard whenever he opened his mouth, which wasn't often. And I jotted down the titles of the books I'd see him with. And soon's I finish up the stack that's by my bed, I'm hitting the library. He started giving me some of the newspapers he keeps stashed in that blue bag of his we all at first thought was full of funky jockstraps and sneakers. Come to find it's full of carrots and oranges and books and stuff. Madeen say he got a gun in there too. But then Madeen all the time saying something. Like she saying here lately that the chemist's jerking off there behind the poisons and the goopher dust.

The chemist's name is Hubert Tarrly. Madeen tagged him Herbert Tareyton. But the name that stuck was Nazi Youth. Every time I look at him I hear Hitler barking out over the loudspeaker urging the youth to measure up and take over the world. And I can see these stark-eyed gray kids in short pants and suspenders doing jump-ups and scissor kicks and turning they mamas in to the Gestapo for listening to the radio. Chemist looks like he grew up like that, eating knockwurst and beating on Jews, rounding up gypsies, saying *Sieg heil* and shit. Mrs. J said something to him one morning and damn if he didn't click his heels. I like to die. She blushing all over her simple self talking bout that's Southern cavalier style. I could smell the gas. I could see the flaming cross too. Nazi Youth and then some. The dude in Drugs started calling him that too, the dude whose name I can never remember. I always wanna say Ali Baba when I talk about him with my girl friends down at the skating rink or with the older sisters at the arts center. But that ain't right. Either you call a person a name that says what they about or you call em what they call themselves, one or the other.

Now take Fur Coat, for instance. She is clearly about the fur coat. She moving up and down the aisles talking while Ethel in the cloth coat is doing all the work, picking up teapots, checking the price on the dust mops, clicking a bracelet against the punch bowl to see if it ring crystal, hollering to somebody about whether the floor wax need buffing or not. And it's all on account of the fur coat. Her work is something other than that. Like when they were in Cosmetics messing with Miz Della, some white ladies come up talking about what's the

latest in face masks. And every time Miz Della pull something
out the box, Ethel shake her head and say that brand is crap.
Then Fur Coat trots out the sure-fire recipe for the face mask.
What she tells the old white ladies is to whip us some egg white
to peaks, pour in some honey, some oil of wintergreen, some
oil of eucalyptus, the juice of a lemon and a half a teaspoon of
arsenic. Now any fool can figure out what lemon juice do to
arsenic, or how honey going make the concoction stick, and
what all else the oil of this and that'll do to your face. But Fur
Coat in her fur coat make you stand still and listen to this
madness. Fur Coat an authority in her fur coat. The fur coat
is an act of alchemy in itself, as Aunt Harriet would put it.

Just like my mama in her fur coat, same kind too—Persian
lamb, bought hot in some riot or other. Mama's coat was part
of the Turn the School Out Outfit. Hardly ever came out of
the quilted bag cept for that. Wasn't for window-shopping,
wasn't for going to rehearsal, wasn't for church teas, was for
working her show. She'd flip a flap of that coat back over her
hip when she strolled into the classroom to get on the teacher's
case bout saying something out of the way about Black folks.
Then she'd pick out the exact plank, exact spot she'd take her
stand on, then plant one of them black suede pumps from the
I. Miller outlet she used to work at. Then she'd lift her chin
arrogant proud to start the rap, and all us kids would lean
forward and stare at the cameo brooch visible now on the
wide-wale wine plush corduroy dress. Then she'd work her
show in her outfit. Bam-bam that black suede pocketbook
punctuating the points as Mama ticked off the teacher's
offenses. And when she got to the good part, and all us kids
would strain up off the benches to hear every word so we could
play it out in the schoolyard, she'd take both fists and brush
that fur coat way back past her hips and she'd challenge the
teacher to either change up and apologize or meet her for a

showdown at a school-board hearing. And of course ole teacher'd apologize to all us Black kids. Then Mama'd let the coat
fall back into place and she'd whip around, the coat draping
like queen robes, and march herself out. Mama was baad in her
fur coat.

I don't know what-all Fur Coat do in her fur coat but I can
tell it's hellafyin whatever it all is. They came into Fabrics and
stood around a while trying to see what shit they could get into.
All they had in their baskets was a teapot and some light bulbs
and some doodads from the special gift department, perfume
and whatnot. I waited on a few customers wanting braid and
balls of macramé twine, nothing where I could show my stuff.
Now if somebody wanted some of the silky, juicy cotton stuff
I could get into something fancy, yanking off the yards, measuring it doing a shuffle-stick number, nicking it just so, then
ripping the hell out the shit. But didn't nobody ask for that.
Fur Coat and Ethel kinda finger some bolts and trade private
jokes, then they moved onto Drugs.

"We'd like to see the latest in rubberized fashions for men,
young man." Fur Coat is doing a super Lady Granville Whit-
more the Third number. "If you would." She bows her head,
fluttering her lashes.

Me and Madeen start messing around in the shoe-polish
section so's not to miss nothing. I kind of favor Fur Coat, on
account of she got my mama's coat on, I guess. On the other
hand, I like the way Ethel drawl talk like she too tired and
bored to go on. I guess I like em both cause they shopping the
right way, having fun and all. And they got plenty of style. I
wouldn't mind being like that when I am full-grown.

The dude in Drugs thinks on the request a while, sucking
in his lips like he wanna talk to himself on the inside. He's
looking up and down the counter, pauses at the plastic rain
hats, rejects them, then squints hard at Ethel and Fur Coat.

Fur Coat plants a well-heeled foot on the shelf with the tampons and pads and sighs. Something about that sigh I don't like. It's real rather than play snooty. The dude in Drugs always looks a little crumbled, a little rough dry, like he jumped straight out the hamper but not quite straight. But he got stuff to him if you listen rather than look. Seems to me ole Fur Coat is looking. She keeps looking while the dude moves down the aisle behind the counter, ducks down out of sight, reappears and comes back, dumping an armful of boxes on the counter.

"One box of Trojans and one box of Ramses," Ethel announces. "We want to do the comparison test."

"On the premises?" Lady G Fur says, planting a dignified hand on her collarbone.

"Egg-zack-lee."

"In your opinion, young man," Lady G Fur says, staying the arm of the brand tester, "which of the two is the best? Uhmm —the better of the two, that is. In your vast experience as lady-killer and cock hound, which passes the X test?" It's said kinda snotty. Me and Madeen exchange a look and dust around the cans of shoe polish.

"Well," the dude says, picking up a box in each hand, "in my opinion, Trojans have a snappier ring to em." He rattles the box against his ear, then lets Ethel listen. She nods approval. Fur Coat will not be swayed. "On the other hand, Ramses is a smoother smoke. Cooler on the throat. What do you say in your vast experience as—er—"

Ethel is banging down boxes of Kotex cracking up, screaming, "He gotcha. He gotcha that time. Old laundry bag got over on you, Helen."

Mrs. J comes out of the prescription booth and hustles her bulk to the counter. Me and Madeen clamp down hard on giggles and I damn near got to climb in with the neutral shoe polish to escape attention. Ethel and Fur Coat don't give a shit, they paying customers, so they just roar. Cept Fur Coat's roar is phony, like she really mad and gonna get even with the dude for not turning out to be a chump. Meanwhile, the dude is standing like a robot, arms out at exactly the same height, elbows crooked just so, boxes displayed between thumb and next finger, the gears in the wrist click, clicking, turning. And not even cracking a smile.

"What's the problem here?" Mrs. J trying not to sound breathless or angry and ain't doing too good a job. She got to say it twice to be heard.

"No problem, Mrs. Johnson," the dude says straight-face. "The customers are buying condoms, I am selling condoms. A sale is being conducted, as is customary in a store."

Mrs. J looks down at the jumble of boxes and covers her mouth. She don't know what to do. I duck down, cause when folks in authority caught in a trick, the first they look for is a scapegoat.

"Well, honey," Ethel says, giving a chummy shove to Mrs. J's shoulder, "what do you think? I've heard that Trojans are ultrasensitive. They use a baby lamb brain, I understand."

"Membrane, dear, membrane," Fur Coat says down her nose. "They remove the intestines of a four-week-old lamb and use the membrane. Tough, resilient, sheer."

"Gotcha," says Ethel. "On the other hand, it is said by folks who should know that Ramses has a better box score."

"Box score," echoes Mrs. J in a daze.

"Box score. You know, honey—no splits, breaks, leaks, seeps."

"Seepage, dear, seepage," says Fur Coat, all nasal.

"Gotcha."

"The solution," says the dude in an almost robot voice, "is to take one small box of each and do the comparison test as you say. A survey. A random sampling of your friends." He says this to Fur Coat, who is not enjoying it all nearly so much as Ethel, who is whooping and hollering.

Mrs. J backs off and trots to the prescription booth. Nazi Youth peeks over the glass and mumbles something soothing to Mrs. J. He waves me and Madeen away like he somebody we got to pay some mind.

"We will take one super-duper, jumbo family size of each."

"Family size?" Fur Coat is appalled. "And one more thing, young man," she orders. "Wrap up a petite size for a small-size smart-ass acquaintance of mine. Gift-wrapped, ribbons and all."

It occurs to me that Fur Coat's going to present this to the dude. Right then and there I decide I don't like her. She's not discriminating with her stuff. Up till then I was thinking how much I'd like to trade Aunt Harriet in for either of these two, hang out with them, sit up all night while they drink highballs and talk about men they've known and towns they've been in. I always did want to hang out with women like this and listen to their stories. But they beginning to reveal themselves as not nice people, just cause the dude is rough dry on Christmas Eve. My Uncle Henry all the time telling me they different kinds of folks in the community, but when you boil it right down there's just nice and not nice. Uncle Henry say they folks who'll throw they mamas to the wolves if the fish sandwich big enough. They folks who won't whatever the hot sauce. They folks that're scared, folks that are dumb; folks that have heart and some with heart to spare. That all boils down to nice and not nice if you ask me. It occurs to me that Fur Coat is not nice. Fun, dazzling, witty, but not nice.

"Do you accept Christmas gifts, young man?" Fur Coat asking in icy tones she ain't masking too well.

"No. But I do accept Kwanza presents at the feast."

"Quan . . . hmm . . ."

Fur Coat and Ethel go into a huddle with the stage whispers. "I bet he thinks we don't know beans about Quantas . . . Don't he know we are The Ebony Jet Set . . . We never travel to kangaroo land except by . . ."

Fur Coat straightens up and stares at the dude. "Will you accept a whatchamacallit gift from me even though we are not feasting, as it were?"

"If it is given with love and respect, my sister, of course." He was sounding so sincere, it kinda got to Fur Coat.

"In that case . . ." She scoops up her bundle and sweeps out the place. Ethel trotting behind hollering, "He gotcha, Helen. Give the boy credit. Maybe we should hire him and do a threesome act." She spun the turnstile round three times for she got into the spin and spun out the store.

"Characters," says Piper on tiptoe, so we all can hear him. He laughs and checks his watch. Madeen slinks over to Tobacco to be in asking distance in case he don't already have a date to the dance. Miz Della's patting some powder on. I'm staring at the door after Fur Coat and Ethel, coming to terms with the fact that my daddy ain't coming. It's gonna be just Uncle Henry and Aunt Harriet this year, with maybe Mama calling on the phone between sets to holler in my ear, asking have I been a good girl, it's been that long since she's taken a good look at me.

"You wanna go to the Kwanza celebrations with me sometime this week or next week, Candy?"

I turn and look at the dude. I can tell my face is falling and right now I don't feel up to doing anything about it. Holidays are depressing. Maybe there's something joyous about this celebration he's talking about. Cause Lord knows Christmas is a drag. The sister who taught me how to wrap a gele asked me was I coming to the celebration down at the Black Arts Center, but I didn't know nothing bout it.

"Look here," I finally say, "would you please get a pencil and paper and write your name down for me. And write that other word down too so I can look it up."

He writes his name down and spins the paper around for me to read.

"Obatale."

"Right," he says, spinning it back. "But you can call me Ali Baba if you want to." He was leaning over too far writing out Kwanza for me to see if that was a smile on his face or a smirk. I figure a smile, cause Obatale nice people.

About the Author

Toni Cade Bambara is author of *The Black Woman, Tales and Short Stories for Black Folks* and *Gorilla, My Love.* Her essays, reviews and short stories have appeared in junior high school texts, literary anthologies, newspapers and magazines. She is now living in Atlanta and is working on a novel.